Bud
- MS
JG

SHADOW
BONES

**Center Point
Large Print**

**This Large Print Book carries the
Seal of Approval of N.A.V.H.**

SHADOW
BONES

COLLEEN RHOADS

CENTER POINT PUBLISHING
THORNDIKE, MAINE

This Center Point Large Print edition
is published in the year 2006 by arrangement with
Harlequin Enterprises, Ltd.

The text of this Large Print edition is unabridged. In other
aspects, this book may vary from the original edition. Printed in
Thailand. Set in 16-point Times New Roman type.

ISBN 1-58547-706-0

Library of Congress Cataloging-in-Publication Data

Rhoads, Colleen.
    Shadow bones / Colleen Rhoads.--Center Point large print ed.
        p. cm.
    ISBN 1-58547-706-0 (lib. bdg. : alk. paper)
        1. Large type books. I. Title.

PS3553.O2285S53 2006
813'.6--dc22

                                                    2006001016

For God hath not given us the spirit of fear;
but of power, and of love, and of a sound mind.
—*II Timothy* 1:7

For New Life Baptist Church
The place I'm most at home this side of heaven

Prologue

Wilson New Moon hummed as he walked through the meadow with his balsam airplane. He loved to watch it soar into the clouds. Sometimes he was tempted to throw it with all his might and see if it could reach heaven.

The preacher said God was in heaven, and Wilson was curious about that. Did God sit on a throne? Did He like balsam planes? A big man, Wilson knew he wasn't smart like other men. He'd once heard a teacher say he'd always have the mental capacity of a twelve-year-old, but Wilson didn't think that was so bad. Twelve was practically an adult.

Wilson knew he wasn't supposed to be here. The mine area was *off-limits*. That's what his mother said. Wilson didn't quite understand what off-limits was, but his mom said the mine was dangerous. He wasn't a scaredy-cat, though. He loved this particular meadow in the springtime. Mushrooms would be popping up any day now. He could take what he found to the hunting shop in town and sell them for enough to buy material to make more planes. This one was getting tattered, and The Sleeping Turtle in town needed more of his creations to sell.

He let the wind take the plane and shouted with exhilaration as it soared on the breeze. Capering in among the wildflowers, he screamed with the wind. He wished he could be a plane himself.

By the middle of the afternoon, he was exhausted. He tucked his plane under his arm. Maybe he should leave it here instead of hauling it to his cabin. Wilson had seen a cave around here somewhere. He scrabbled through the underbrush.

There it was. He uprooted a shrub and revealed the opening back into the mine. It was bigger than he remembered—big enough for him to explore.

Smiling hugely, he got on all fours and crawled inside. This could be his hiding place. He could play tricks on other mushroom hunters from here and scare them away.

He heard a sound, and his blood boomed in his ears. He looked behind him and saw a black face atop a figure dressed in black. White teeth bared, the creature reached for him.

A scream tore from his throat, and Wilson backpedaled as quick as he could. It was Asibikaashi, the Spider Woman. Weaver of dreamcatchers, Asibikaashi had always terrified Wilson. Though the Ojibwa were encouraged to protect and revere her, he wanted nothing to do with anything that had eight legs.

The shriek that issued from his mouth hurt his ears. He turned and ran for his life. Every moment he expected to feel the silken thread of the Spider Woman's web entangle him and the sharp sting of her teeth entering his back. He didn't dare look behind him as he ran for safety.

Chapter One

"Mother, what were you thinking?" Skye Blackbird wanted to stamp her size seven foot and proclaim this a hill she would die on, but one look at her mother's face convinced her she'd be left bleeding on the hillside.

She fought back the impulse to burst into tears. This was her father's dream—and her own—that was about to vanish. Her mother had to listen to reason.

She jerkily tied a knot in the dreamcatcher on her lap, but not even keeping her hands busy kept her emotions from churning her stomach into knots.

Her shop, The Sleeping Turtle, was empty of customers this beautiful May morning. But even if tourists had packed the narrow aisles filled with herbs and Ojibwa paraphernalia, she wouldn't have been able to hold her tongue. Luckily, the bulk of tourists wouldn't be riding the ferry out to Eagle Island for another month. Then the small island in Lake Superior would be burgeoning with sightseers.

Mary Metis, Skye's mother, tucked one black lock behind her ear. "You're not being reasonable, Skye. Letting the man look for dinosaur bones won't hurt the running of the mine. I don't tell you how to operate your business, so don't tell me how to manage mine. I get enough of that from Peter." Her voice vibrated with suppressed anger.

Skye hurried to smooth things over. "Are you mad at Peter? He's just trying to look out for you."

"I'm not a child."

"You're just ticked at him right now," Skye responded. "Peter has been good to you and to me. He always knows what's best."

"The mine belongs to me, not to you or Peter," her mother went on. "It's about time I start taking back some of the decision-making about it."

"But you don't even know these people," Skye protested. "We know nothing about them."

That wasn't exactly true, and she knew it. This paleontologist, Jake Baxter, was Mrs. Baxter's grandson. The Baxters had practically owned the entire island for years, though that knowledge did nothing to endear the man to Skye. She liked things to stay the same.

"We've known the Baxters for years," her mother said. "I don't understand your attitude. Jake Baxter merely wants to poke around a bit, see if he can dig up any bones."

Skye hadn't met this particular Baxter yet, but she already disliked him. "We've always been told some of The Old Ones are buried on our property. What if Jake disturbs their bones?"

"On *my* property," Mary said. She laid down a bundle of dried chives, tied with twine. The pungent odor permeated the shop and mingled with that of chamomile, comfrey, mint and other herbs.

"Okay, on your property. And besides, I've been running the garnet mine for you for the past four years. I think I should have some say. I can just see people swarming all over the place and disrupting the operation of the mine."

"He'll be on the slope, not actually in the mine," her mother pointed out.

Skye finally voiced her real objection. She didn't even want to think about it. "And what happens if he finds something important? He could close us down while he digs. Permanently! I'll never find the diamonds if that happens."

Her mother's face softened, and she reached out to touch Skye's face with gentle fingers. "Skye, there are no diamonds. Your father combed every inch of that mine in his search and found nothing. I often think that disappointment was what drove him away."

Skye knew better. If she'd been a better daughter, her father wouldn't have left. If she could find the diamonds, maybe he'd hear of it and come back. "Please reconsider," she said in a low voice that quivered, no matter how much she tried to keep it steady.

"Let it go, Skye. This is just for the summer. Jake will be gone before you know it." Mary fished a sheaf of herbs out of the basket by her feet and began to prepare another bundle.

"That's what he's telling you, but I have a bad feeling about this." Skye hung the finished dreamcatcher in the window beside the others she'd completed so far this month.

Dreams, that's what some would say was all she had in this shop, and that was all she would ever have. But she'd prayed and prayed for this shop, and she wasn't ready to give up on it yet.

"You'll see what a nice man he is for yourself," Mary said. "I want you to run an errand for me this morning and go see Jake."

"I need to watch the shop." The last thing Skye wanted was to see the man face-to-face.

"I'll watch it. I told Jake I'd have you bring out the lease for him to sign."

Skye almost couldn't speak. "You're giving him a *lease?* Mother, please don't do this."

Her mother set her jaw. "I have already agreed to it, Skye. I'm a woman of my word."

"Peter won't like it, either." Skye crossed her arms over her chest. Peter would talk sense into her mother. He'd apologize for whatever tiff had caused this problem.

"We've already discussed it, and I'm not changing my mind. The more the two of you hound me, the more determined I am to do what I think best. I'm not a child, Skye, though you and Peter like to treat me that way."

Her mother sounded on the verge of tears, and Skye decided to back off. Her mother had been fragile ever since her husband, Skye's father, had walked out on them eight years ago when Skye was sixteen. If not for Peter, Skye didn't know how she would have dealt with all of it. But even he knew better than to cross his wife when she was this set on a course of action.

Skye leaned back against the chair and rubbed her forehead. "How long is the lease?"

"Just for the summer." Her mother's voice held a

trace of smugness. She leaned down and pulled a handful of papers from her purse and gave them to Skye.

Skye took them, glancing through the terms. "This clause says he can extend the lease if he finds something of significance to science." She wanted to fling the lease in the trash and set it afire.

Her mother shrugged her slim shoulders. "You can't seriously think he'll find anything here. It's a summer pastime for Jake, nothing more."

Skye had heard of Jake Baxter's expertise in the field. He wouldn't be wasting his time if he didn't expect to find something. "Look at this clause, Mother. At least change it," she pleaded. "Make it for the summer only with no extension."

Her mother hesitated. "If I do, will you quit fighting me on it?"

Skye bit her lip. She wasn't sure she could hold her tongue. "All right," she said.

"Fine." Her mother took a pen and crossed out the clause then initialed it. "I want you to go out now," she said, handing the papers back to Skye.

Skye nearly groaned, but she rose instead. "Where do I find him?"

"On the southwest slope."

"That's my favorite spot! I love to walk through the wildflowers there. He's going to ruin my whole summer."

"Skye, show a little graciousness," Mary called after her as Skye stormed from the store.

13

Skye climbed in her 1962 Dodge pickup. Though the paint didn't shine anymore and the seats were cracked, she felt close to her father in this truck. He'd restored it once upon a time, but he'd left it behind like a discarded toy. Just like he'd left his family.

But she would never leave this island as he did. Her mother needed her, and Skye needed the blue twilight in Lake Superior's depths on a lazy summer afternoon. She needed the way the sun glinted off the white cliffs in the winter and the harsh sound of the gulls fighting for a morsel of fish. This land was in her blood, just like it had been in her ancestors'. She was her father's daughter, the daughter of an Ojibwa chieftain. But she would prove more faithful than he.

The truck's tires kicked up a cloud of dust behind her, and the back end fishtailed on the gravel road. She realized she was clenching the steering wheel so hard her fingers were numb. Her jaw ached, and she forced herself to try to relax. She wanted to appear calm and in control when she tried to talk Jake Baxter into giving up this crazy scheme.

The mine was ten miles out of town. Surrounded by pine forests interspersed with stands of white birch, the garnet mine had been her focus ever since she took over management three years ago. She pulled into the parking lot in front of the mine. Two other vehicles were parked there. She'd never seen either one of them. The beat-up truck was probably his. It held picks and other digging tools.

She got out of her vehicle and slammed the door

behind her with more force than necessary, though the action failed to relieve the tension coiled in her gut.

Following the trail of crushed wildflowers, she stalked up the slope to the site her mother had told her Jake intended to dig up. The path to the meadow was always dangerous, as it narrowed to only a foot wide at its steepest, most treacherous part, and in her state of mind, it was hard to take the care she should.

As she neared the rocky outcropping, she could hear the murmur of voices. The man's deep voice sent an odd thrill up her spine, a reaction that made her grit her teeth.

She paused to assess the enemy before stepping around the final boulder barring her way.

Jake Baxter stood with his feet planted on the ground as though he owned it. A red denim shirt and well-worn jeans outlined his tall, rangy form. Skye's gaze traveled from his scuffed boots to the Indiana Jones-style hat that topped his shaggy black hair. The man had to be at least six-four.

He stood tossing a rock from hand to hand like a quarterback would play with a football. The woman on his left wore the same determined expression, and her dark hair matched Jake's. The other woman was blond and blue-eyed, the antithesis of the other two, and Skye recognized her as Becca Duncan, who frequented her shop.

The three stood deep in conversation, then Becca turned and saw her. "Skye, I'm glad you've come out. You've never met my brother and sister."

When Jake turned and his dark eyes focused on her face, Skye wanted to run. Even from here, she could see the determination in his jaw and the piercing expression in eyes the color of the walnut trees that grew in the forest.

He wouldn't intimidate her. She lifted her chin and stepped from behind the rock. "Hello, Becca." Her tone measured, she advanced to the stone outcropping.

Jake's gaze swept her and rested on her face. "You're Skye Blackbird? Somehow I'd pictured someone dressed in gauzy skirts and wearing crystals around her neck."

"Oh?" At least her linen slacks were still spotless. She smoothed her red jacket over her hips.

"I've heard you're the island medicine woman. You look too much like a modern woman to believe in herbs and roots."

"A typically uninformed comment. God created everything in this world for a purpose. If we give our bodies the natural substances God made for us, we'd all be a lot better off. Even an Indiana Jones-type like you."

Instead of the comment irritating him as she'd planned, he grinned, a lazy smile full of self-confidence. "I'm glad you noticed."

Skye gritted her teeth but managed to keep silent.

"You look mad enough to kick a boulder in two," Jake said. "Was it something I said?" His grin widened.

Becca's smile faltered. "You okay, Skye?"

"No, no, I'm not." Skye folded her arms over her

chest. She narrowed her gaze and glared at Jake. "I've brought the lease, but only under duress. I'd like to persuade you to abandon the idea of digging here. You'll disrupt my mining and destroy the environment in this area. There are other, less fragile, places on the island to dig. I suggest you look around."

She tossed out the final comment with a challenging tilt to her chin.

Jake shoved his hands in his pockets, and the amusement in his eyes died. "It's not that easy."

His deep drawl raised Skye's hackles even more. "Sure it is," she said. "You pack up this equipment and saunter off to some place that wants you."

"I have a feeling about this spot," Jake said. "If I'm right, it could be a huge discovery. I'm sorry you don't approve, but your mother *has* given her permission. She owns the land, so I don't think you have anything to say about it." The final sentence was uttered with a gentleness that didn't quite extend to the grim look in his eyes.

Heat rushed to Skye's cheeks, and her jaw ached from clenching her teeth. "Don't get in the way of my workers," she snapped.

"I don't intend to. Now if you'll give me that contract, I can sign it and get to work."

"Mother made a change." She dropped her backpack, flipped it open and then pulled out the lease. She wanted to crumple it into a ball and toss it over the cliff, but she forced an impassive glare and handed it to Jake.

Skye pointed out the crossed out clause. "The lease is

17

for the summer only with no extension."

Jake sighed. He took off his hat and rubbed his forehead. "That's not acceptable to me. We had an agreement." He pulled his cell phone out of his pocket and dialed. "Mrs. Metis? Jake Baxter here. I really need that clause in the lease. I can't jeopardize the dig with time constraints, and you gave me your word."

As soon as she heard his cajoling voice and the way he reminded her mother of her promise, Skye knew her mother would cave. Mary Metis prided herself on being a woman of her word. Besides, Jake had a way of presenting his view that seemed so plausible.

He handed her the phone, and she listened while her mother told her to reinstate the clause. Skye knew better than to argue. Nothing was more important to her mother than her word.

She clicked off the phone and handed it back to Jake. She crossed out the correction her mother had made, though it pained her to do so.

"May I borrow your pen?"

For a moment she was tempted to tell him no, but that would just delay the inevitable. She held out a pen without saying anything.

Jake took it and signed the lease with a flourish. "Thank your mother for her willingness to advance science."

"So you've won," she said, her voice clipped.

Jake shrugged, and Skye felt her temper rise.

"I'd like to think we'll all win," Jake said, with a disarming smile. "I'm not your enemy. Your mom makes a little money, and we might all discover something to benefit mankind."

"What benefit is a bunch of bones?" She knew she was being argumentative, but the man's confidence needed shaking up.

"What benefit are garnets?"

"Are you always so condescending?" Skye couldn't hold back the words.

Becca gave a nervous chuckle. "Jake, be nice."

Jake gave his sister a wounded look. "I'm being nice. But how are gems worth more than the history of life on earth?"

With Jake's gaze on her, Skye couldn't muster a single one of the arguments she'd thought of on the way out here. For the first time, she questioned the value of her determination to find diamonds in her mine. At the end of life, they really would be worthless. Was she chasing something that held no real value?

But even Jake's vaunted scientific discovery would be nothing when standing before God's throne. And her motives weren't about money anyway.

She pressed her lips together and stuffed her copy of the lease back into her purse and handed Jake the other copy. "It looks like I have no choice."

The petite, dark-haired woman smiled and held out her hand. "No one seems disposed to introduce us. I'm Wynne Baxter. Becca was a Baxter before she married, but it seems we're still stuck with Jake. Kidding aside, he is actually very conscious of the environment when he works a dig. I think you'll be pleasantly surprised

19

how little he'll disturb the area."

The knot in Skye's stomach uncoiled a bit by the young woman's friendly manner. In different circumstances they might be friends. "I find that hard to believe."

Wynne fell into step beside her, and they walked toward Skye's truck. "It's going to be okay, Skye. Jake will be careful. You'll see."

Skye felt near tears and wasn't sure why. She felt as if Jake had made her appear to be a willful child. "Why did he have to pick this spot?" She didn't want to see the beauty of her favorite meadow destroyed.

"He saw some rock shapes he thought might mean something. I doubt it will take long for him to move on to another place. By the end of the summer, he'll be out of your hair." Wynne opened the door of Skye's truck for her.

Skye managed a smile. "Thanks, Wynne. I'll try to ignore him."

"I think you and Jake could be friends."

"I doubt that," Skye said as Wynne turned to rejoin her siblings.

Jake squinted in the bright sunshine. He stood at the top of the slope and looked out on the green swell of forest. Below him was the entrance to the mine, and behind him he could see Turtle Town, ten miles distant.

He'd always wanted to dig on this island. Something about it called to him, a siren song that whispered of secrets and treasures too vast and unusual to imagine.

And finding these rocks with the intriguing shapes added to his hunch.

Such fancies haunted his dreams and drove him on in his profession as a paleontologist. There was no telling where or when the earth might yield the next discovery, revealing new knowledge, new horizons. The oddly shaped rocks in this area just might mean a dinosaur nursery, which could wipe away his earlier failure.

Too bad Skye Blackbird was so opposed to his presence here. Jake had a feeling she could show him parts of the island no one else had ever seen.

"This looks like a good spot to get started," he said. An ocean of wildflowers swam in his vision. Daisies, poppies, black-eyed Susans. He wondered how even God painted with such a palette of colors.

"Mary said we could set up camp anywhere we wanted," Becca said.

"How about at Windigo Manor?" Wynne asked hopefully. "I'm tired of roughing it. Jake, you should be, too. I don't know what possessed you to suggest camping. Don't you get enough of that on a dig?"

"I hardly know how to sleep in a real bed anymore," Jake said. "I like to sleep out under the stars." His heavy work boots crushed the pine needles strewn along the path, and he inhaled the fresh scent with gusto. While he'd enjoyed his stint in Montserrat, there was no place like Michigan's Upper Peninsula. Eagle Island, just off the shore of the Keweenaw Peninsula was the place he loved best. He relished the thought of finally being able to explore this island.

He shook his head at his sisters. "You know we'll have to deal with security issues. That's easier if I'm staying on site."

Wynne rolled her eyes. "Who would bother things on this tiny island? I think you're worrying unnecessarily."

Newly married Becca stopped to pick a wild rose growing along the path. He grinned at the dreamy expression on her face. Jake had gotten a charge out of watching his sister with her new husband. The normally reticent Becca had bloomed under Max's love and care.

Wynne nodded at Becca. "True love is beautiful. It's your turn next, Jake."

"Yeah, right. No woman alive would put up with me and my schedule."

"Maybe it's time you thought about staying in one place, settling down."

"That's no way to make a name in my field."

"That's not the real reason, is it?" Wynne said gently. "You still feel you have to prove yourself. When will you stop beating yourself up over that earlier discovery? It wasn't your fault."

"Any graduate student should have recognized that find as a fraud, Wynne. You're not the one who sees interest change to amusement when people hear my name." He still felt sick when he remembered dating what he'd thought was a huge find and then discovering it was a hoax perpetrated by three teenagers in England.

Wynne patted his arm. "We all make mistakes, Jake."

"Well, I want to wipe this one away," he said grimly. He forced a smile. "And you have no room to talk about settling down. You're just as bad. Where was it you were last—Italy?"

"So?" Wynne shrugged her slim shoulders. "Maybe I'm holding out for someone in my own field who will travel with me. I'm not as competitive as you."

That was a pipe dream. She'd never find someone like that, Jake thought.

"What a beautiful spot." Wynne paused in a clearing dusted with wildflowers. A steep slope rose behind the clearing, and from here he could see the opening to the mine. "What's that place called?" Jake asked his youngest sister.

"Turtle Mountain." Becca stopped and plucked a Shasta daisy.

"I'd like to tour the mine sometime," Wynne said. "I've never seen a garnet mine."

"Skye seems to think she's going to run into diamonds any day now." Becca seemed serious.

Jake laughed. "Diamonds in the UP? Is she nuts?" She hadn't looked crazy. Skye Blackbird had a cool, elegant look that intrigued him. He supposed any man would wonder what made her tick. She was beautiful in a Sleeping Beauty kind of way. Her high Ojibwa cheekbones were sharp enough to draw blood from a man's heart. He didn't intend to let her close enough to see if she could hurt him.

"In her defense, there are some signs it could be possible."

"Oh?"

"Her stepfather, Peter Metis, has been pouring money

23

into the mine and even hired an assayer a couple of weeks ago. He's pretty savvy, so I doubt he'd be doing that without a good reason."

"Have I met him?"

"Not unless you've taken out a loan lately. He is the president at the bank in Turtle Town."

"He's Ojibwa, too?"

Becca nodded. "According to town scuttlebutt, he took over the bank—and the Blackbird women—when Harry deserted his family."

"Skye's father?" Wynne's voice was full of sympathy.

"Skye was pretty broken up about it, from what I hear. She hasn't trusted a man since then." Becca cast a slanting glance up into Jake's face. "You could show her all men aren't beasts."

"I doubt I'll get close enough to get the chance," he said shortly. "And I don't want to."

Chapter Two

Jake had thought to find something by now. He wiped his forehead with a bandana that had seen better days. Wynne wrinkled her nose. "All you're doing is smearing the dirt around," she said.

Jake ignored her comment as he squatted over the dig. "A week into this, and nothing." He'd had a hunch about this place, but he was beginning to wonder if he'd been seduced by the island's beauty.

"Did you expect to find something this fast?"

24

"You know me—I always expect the best."

"And seldom get it," she pointed out.

Jake grinned and stood. "How about some lunch?"

"Sounds good." Wynne trotted to the cooler they'd parked under a nearby rock.

The rumble of a car engine drew Jake's attention. He squinted in the brilliant sun. A blue pickup rolled to a stop in the road. A woman got out of the passenger side. Jake's stomach tightened as a familiar figure got out the driver side.

"Cameron Reynolds," he muttered.

"You're kidding!" Wynne went to Jake's side and looked down the slope to the road. "What's he doing here?" Her voice was tight.

"I'd say we're about to find out." Jake took out his pocket watch and glanced at it. "I'll give him fifteen minutes, then I'm throwing him off the site."

Cameron wore immaculate khaki trousers and a light blue shirt. His blond hair formed a pale cap around his angular face. Cameron was the type of man Jake despised most: a dabbling pretty boy who thought their field of study existed to amuse him. He liked to flash his money around, too—another thing that put Jake's back up after scrabbling for sponsors all his life.

Cameron was the very antithesis of a real paleontologist.

Cameron came up the slope toward them. He didn't bother to help the woman trailing him. Jake didn't trust the genial smile on the man's face. "What are you doing here, Reynolds?"

25

Cameron put his hand up as if to ward off the hostility in Jake's voice. "Whoa, Jake, I come in peace." He chuckled at his own joke.

Jake didn't find it funny. "Don't make any Native American jokes around here, or the owner will toss you off the reservation on your ear. On second thought, go right ahead. She'll save me the bother."

"Hey, come on, guy. We can at least be civil."

"Why? The last time you showed up, you horned in on my dig and took the credit for the T-Rex fossils I found." Jake folded his arms over his chest.

"I mentioned your name in the article. Besides, you need my respectability." He tossed Jake a smirk then jerked his head toward the woman. "This is my assistant, Brook Sawyer."

She was in her twenties, Jake judged. She nodded at them then looked down at the ground and didn't speak. Jake nodded back then stared pointedly at Cameron. "Don't throw me any bones." He jerked his head toward his dig. "I suppose you want to cut in on the action here. No way."

"I figure if you're wasting your whole summer here, you've got a really good reason." Cameron looked around, his face alive with curiosity.

"My family is here. I'm just killing time while I visit with them."

Cameron chuckled. "Forgive me if I don't believe that." He slanted a glance toward Wynne. "You're just as beautiful as ever, Wynne."

Wynne smiled but there was no warmth in the expression. "Hello, Cameron. Just as smarmy as ever, I see."

"Smarmy? That was a sincere compliment. How about dinner one night?" Cameron's smile never dimmed.

"Don't you think you'd better scope out the other possibilities first?" Wynne's eyes were hostile.

Jake was glad to see she hadn't forgotten the way Cameron had wined and dined her then dropped her when a more ripe candidate had come along.

"Come on, forgive and forget, Wynne. You can show me the sights." He took her hand.

"I'd be more apt to tip you over a cliff into Superior." Wynne pulled her hand free. "I'd better get lunch ready." She turned and walked away from the men.

Jake grinned at the way she put Cameron in his place. "How did you figure out where I was?"

"A little birdie told me," Cameron said, his eyes still on Wynne. He sighed then walked to the dig and squatted.

"Careful, you might wrinkle your pants." Jake was suddenly tired of the sparring.

"We were partners a long time, Jake. I think it's time you got over the personal stuff."

"I don't trust you, Reynolds. This is my dig. I don't need your help."

Cameron flicked a paper out of his pocket. "The owner says differently."

Jake's face tightened as he read the lease from Mary Metis. She'd granted Reynolds permission to dig out here, too, but farther out from this site. "How'd you get around her? Did you tell her we were partners once?"

"Something like that."

Jake wanted to wipe the smug grin off Cameron's face. "You stay out of my dig, Reynolds. Go poke around on your own side of the slope. This spot's mine."

"We'd be better off to pool our resources," Cameron suggested. He glanced around. "I know what you're onto here."

Jake's stomach tightened. He had to get rid of Cameron before he saw anything more. "Not going to happen." Jake glanced at his watch. "I need to get back to work. You can find your own way off my site."

"If this really is a baby dinosaur nest, you need my help."

"I'm perfectly capable of making any discoveries on my own," Jake said. He stared at Cameron until he shrugged and turned toward the path down to the truck. His assistant followed him. Jake joined his sister.

"Is this going to be trouble?" Wynne asked. She handed him a sandwich. "It's peanut butter. There's milk in the Thermos."

Jake unwrapped it. "Might be. It's a good thing I'm sleeping out here."

"Is he that desperate?"

"That's how he's climbing the ladder—on the backs of other paleontologists. One of these days someone is going to kill him over it."

Wynne shuddered. "Don't talk like that."

"It's the truth. He's a barracuda."

28

"But a cute one," Wynne noted.

Jake wrinkled his nose. "I thought you were over him."

"I am, but I'm not blind, either." Wynne laughed and took a bite of her sandwich. "Maybe I should do a little hobnobbing with the enemy and see what he's up to."

"I don't want you within ten feet of that snake." Jake looked in her face and saw the wheels turning. "No way, Wynne! Don't even think about it. You're not in the same league with him. He already discarded you once."

Wynne sniffed. "I can handle myself. I'm not a little girl, Jake."

"You won't have time to waste on the likes of Reynolds." Jake knew he'd get nowhere by ordering Wynne around. She'd always been the independent type. "Let's get back to work."

She downed the last swallow of milk and crumpled the paper cup in her hand, then tossed it in the plastic trash bag. "Okay, lead on, fearless one."

Jake just hoped she'd forget about Cameron Reynolds.

They worked all afternoon in the hot sun. The breeze they'd enjoyed earlier in the week seemed to have evaporated like Superior's morning mist. The drone of insects and the scraping of their tools had a lulling effect on him, and he had to fight to keep his attention on the task at hand.

About four, he hit something. Using his fingers, he carefully began to clean the spot away. The task was painstaking and tedious in the hard clay dirt. The hole widened. A few more minutes and he'd have the object free. By five, a large egg-shaped rock lay exposed. Jake tried to still the flutters of excitement in his belly as he saw other possible eggs under the top one. The find confirmed his hunch about the rounded shapes in the stones around him.

"I think we've done it," he said, settling in to dig up more and make sure.

The bell tinkled on the door to The Sleeping Turtle. From her position on a ladder with herbs in her hands, Skye couldn't see the customer. "I'll be with you in just a minute," she called.

She heard quick steps and glanced around. Before she could tell who had come in, the ladder began to shake. Skye grabbed hold and hung on.

"You'll pay for what you've done!"

Skye craned her neck and looked down. Tallulah Levenger, a frequent customer, gripped the ladder rails with both hands. Her brows drawn together, she looked savage. Her salt-and-pepper hair hung in strings around her face, and she was still dressed in her nightgown.

Skye clung to the ladder with both hands. She felt dizzy and disoriented from the shaking. For a moment, she thought Tallulah would toss the ladder onto its side with Skye still attached. Poised on her right leg, Skye let go and leaped for the floor. Better to choose her own landing.

She slammed to the wooden floor with a force that

buckled her legs. Her knees stung from the impact with the hard wood, and a wave of pain radiated from her left knee. She groaned as she heard cursing behind her. She needed to get up and face whatever had caused this, but she found it hard to move, hard to think.

She grabbed hold of a nearby table and staggered to her feet, wincing at the pain in her left knee. Holding out her hands in a placating manner, she tried to calm Tallulah. "Tallulah, what's wrong?"

The veins stood out in Tallulah's neck. Her eyes were narrowed to slits. She advanced toward Skye. "You killed him!" She came at Skye's neck with hands curled into claws, then leaped onto her, and they both tumbled to the floor.

Skye could smell the unwashed odor that emanated from Tallulah. The woman's breath stank as she grappled with Skye on the wooden floor. Tallulah's hands tightened on Skye's throat.

The pressure made Skye gag, and she fought to catch her breath. She tried to pry the fingers loose, but Tallulah just pressed harder. Dark spots danced in Skye's vision, and she gasped for air. She finally managed to pry one finger loose and bent it back until the woman released her.

Skye rolled away and sprang to her feet. She put a table display of painted stones between them.

Tallulah stood with her hands clenched. Her chest rose and fell in heaves. "Murderer! Witch! Those herbs you gave me didn't work." She started toward Skye again.

Skye backed away. "Are you talking about Robert?" Her stomach roiled. Robert was dead? She shuddered. The teenager was one of her favorites, and she remembered the listless air he'd had when his mother brought him in. His coloring had been pasty as well.

"You killed him." Tears rolled down Tallulah's face, and she covered her face with her hands.

Skye wanted to comfort her, but she didn't dare get too close. "Did you take him to the doctor like I told you? The herbs just enhance health, they won't cure someone who is that sick."

"I don't hold with doctors. If you'd given me the right herbs, he'd still be alive." The bereaved mother wept and pulled on her hair. "It's all your fault." She started toward Skye, who moved to keep the table between them.

"I gave you what you asked for, but I told you to take him to the doctor. What happened?"

"A ruptured appendix, they say." Tallulah's face twisted with grief. "Then gangrene."

"Oh, no. I told you I thought it was his appendix." Skye's knees threatened to buckle. Could she have done more to save the boy? She'd begged Tallulah to take the teen to the hospital. Maybe she should have called someone.

"Don't try to blame me. It's your fault. And I'm going to make sure you pay." Tallulah bared her teeth, then turned and plunged down an aisle toward the door.

Skye drew a deep breath when she heard the door slam. She reached out and grabbed the side of the table with shaking hands. Everyone in town talked about Tallulah, but this had been her first experience with the woman's uglier side.

She rubbed her throat. The sheriff should be told about this, but she didn't have the heart to get the other woman in trouble. She'd lost her son, and anyone would be a little unhinged.

Shaken more than she wanted to admit, she fixed a cup of chamomile tea and went to the window seat that looked out on her back garden. She sipped it until her nerves settled. Good thing her mother hadn't been here. Mother would have fainted.

Glancing at her watch, she realized she had just enough time to check in with the mine's manager, James Manomen. She drove out to the mine and parked beside Jake's SUV.

She had tried to avoid the place until she adjusted to the thought of what the paleontologist was doing out here, yet being present caused a physical ache. She turned her gaze away from the sight of Jake working with Wynne and two other men.

The mine opening yawned in the side of the wild-flower-covered hillside. She stepped to the entrance. Inside, lights strung along the sloping sides illuminated the tunnel she walked down. She felt cold, as cold as the water dripping along the floor of the mine, and wished she'd brought a jacket. Inside the mine, it was always around fifty-five degrees, and the damp had a way of permeating one's bones.

Her manager crouched over a massive drill. Her

cousin, Michael Blackbird, stood over him holding a light, and the drill operator stood off to one side.

"Problems, Pop?" she asked.

A big Ojibwa, the manager James Manomen wore his black hair in a single long braid down his back. In his forties, he'd been like another father to Skye for more years than she could count. Calling him Pop helped fill a void in her life.

James shook his head. "I've repaired it." He straightened and punched the button to restart the drill. The engine rumbled to life, and the noise was near deafening.

"Let's go to my office," Skye shouted.

James and Michael nodded and followed her down the corridor to the office. Michael shut the rusting metal door behind him. The door muffled the sound of the drill down to a dull roar. "I have high hopes for this tube," he said.

Her cousin's face was grimy with grease. He reminded her of her father with a white wing of gray hair on the right side of his black hair. About forty, he was the only son of Skye's Uncle Louis and was the only other member of the family to work at the mine. She'd never been close to him since he was so much older.

Skye's fingers tightened on the coffee cup in her hand. "You really think this could be it?"

He nodded. "You're the first one who noticed the kimberlites. Surely, you're not losing hope now."

"The kimberlites don't always mean diamonds." She

didn't want to admit how discouraged she felt today. The kimberlites were special rocks that were often found in conjunction with diamonds. She could only hope and pray that was the case here.

"No, but you've never lost faith that the stones are here," James put in.

"We've been searching for two years, James." Her voice sounded weary, even to herself. "We're running out of money."

"Ask Peter for more. He'll do anything for you," Michael said.

"I can't keep taking handouts from him. At some point, I'm either going to have to find the diamonds or admit defeat. The assayer he hired a couple of weeks ago found nothing." She handed him a cup of coffee then poured one for James.

James's eyes widened as he took the coffee she offered him. "I've never heard you talk like this. What's wrong?"

She plopped into the old chair at the metal desk. "Am I fooling myself, guys? I've been chasing this dream so long I'm not sure anymore. Sometimes a dream is just that. I might have to face reality."

Michael sat in one of the chairs. Her cousin was the only one of her father's relatives her mother still had contact with. His father, Louis Blackbird, never worked more than a couple of months out of any year, and he blamed Mary for the way his brother had run off. A big man weighing nearly two hundred and seventy pounds, Michael's sturdy strength was a constant source of support for Skye.

He propped his feet up on the desk. "Has someone been talking to you?"

Skye hesitated. "Mother is ready to shut down the mine."

"It still produces garnets," he pointed out. "This is our livelihood, Skye."

"Yes, but we're losing money. We can't continue at this rate. I see her point." James took a sip of coffee and grimaced. "I think this must have been made this morning."

"I want to try the Mitchell tube," Michael said.

"Peter doesn't want us to go there. He says it's too dangerous." Skye had wanted to work in that tube for years, but her stepfather had forbidden the venture. She knew the tube wasn't safe, but part of her longed to chance it.

"We could shore up the walls," James suggested.

"It would cost too much." She sighed and took the last swig of coffee and rose. "I have to get out of here for a while."

"Take tomorrow off," Michael urged. "You've been working too hard at the shop, spreading yourself thin with worry. After a little rest, you'll be your old self again."

"I still have to face facts," she said. Her steps dragging, she went past James and Michael and left the office, then turned down the corridor and stepped outside into the bright sunshine. She cocked her head as the sound of distant whoops and shouts echoed from the slope to her left. Frowning, she turned to see what the commotion was about.

Slipping and sliding on the loose rocks, she hurried along the path to the dig. At the top of the hill, she could see Jake twirling his sister around and around. They were both shouting. The other two workers were peering over the edge of the hole at something. Not good. Skye felt a sinking sensation in her stomach. She made her way to the dig.

"What's going on?" she demanded.

Jake turned, and his hands dropped to his sides. The elation on his face radiated a charm she wasn't prepared for. Skye felt an invisible wall go up. He took a step toward her, and she backed away.

The joy on his face diminished a few watts. "Look here." He gestured toward some egg-shaped rocks.

"So?" She dismissed the rocks with a glance.

"We've found a dinosaur nesting site." Jake nearly chortled with glee. He rubbed his hands together.

"What does that mean?" Skye had a dismal feeling it wouldn't be news she wanted to hear.

"Do you have any idea how rare a nesting site is?" His voice rose. "This is the find of the century."

All her worst fears rose up to smack her in the face. The media would be on this like a frog on a June bug. Damage control, she thought frantically. How did she minimize the effect this would have on her mining operation?

"You're not saying anything." The light in Jake's eyes faded even more.

"You have to keep this quiet," she said.

His dark brows winged up. "Quiet? The entire pale-ontology community will be interested in this find."

"And I'll lose the mine," she said. She felt like she was choking. It was one thing to talk about giving up her dream and something else to have it forced on her.

It was time she faced the fact she would never find the diamonds. The Turtle Mine was just an aging garnet mine, not a diamond mine.

And her father was never coming back.

She felt the sting of tears and turned away. Jake's breath whispered against her neck, and his warm hands touched her arms.

"I'm sorry," he said.

The funny thing was she believed he really did regret what his find would do to her business. Her mom's business, she corrected herself. Her mother didn't care, so Skye should just let it go. So why couldn't she do just that?

"Do you have to announce it yet?" she asked in a small voice. Her gaze stayed on the ground in front of her.

For a few moments she thought Jake wasn't going to answer. His grip slackened. "We can delay it a while. But I'm going to need help to fully excavate the site."

She pulled away then turned and gazed into his face. "What about the other paleontologist who's working the other site? He could help you."

He grimaced. "I can't do that."

"He seems congenial."

"Oh, he's congenial right up to the point where he'll treat your stuff as his own. He's also two-faced and greedy. He'll be sure to announce the find so it looks like it was his baby." He shook his head. "I'll find some help in town."

"So it's all about power and fame for you? What about the devastation you leave behind you?" She gestured to the hillside. "There won't be much left of this hill, will there? By the time you all get through, it will be an open grave."

His lips pressed into a straight line. "This is more important than the paltry amount of garnets you're likely to find in this old mine."

"It's not garnets I'm looking for," she burst out.

"Diamonds." Amusement lit his dark eyes. "What a pipe dream."

"About as likely as finding a dinosaur nursery, right?" She heard the challenge in her voice and lifted her head. She wasn't going to give up without a fight.

A dull red crept up his neck and touched his cheeks. "Touché," he said. "This is about knowledge and our history. It's much more important than diamonds."

"To whom? I'm not looking for diamonds for the money."

"Then what's the motive?" He took off his hat and rubbed his hand through his hair.

"You wouldn't understand." She didn't bother to hide the contempt in her voice. There was no getting through his thick head. She wasn't sure she understood it herself. Her rational side knew finding the diamonds wouldn't bring her father back, but she still clung to the hope that he'd walk back through that door.

Chapter Three

Jake worked for three days on further excavation. He longed to call the media and rejoice in his find, but he restrained himself after promising Skye to keep a lid on it for now. This was everything he'd been working toward all his life. He would no longer be remembered as the scientist who was duped by a bunch of high school kids. As he unearthed more and more eggs, his smile grew larger.

He took Sunday off and went to church with his family. They were always nagging him about church. He wished he could join worship with the same joy he used to feel. The stark truth was that since his parents had been killed, he blamed God. And that was hard to get past.

He felt God constantly pressing him to let go of the anger and hurt, but it had been impossible for him to get past. He slid into the pew and felt the atmosphere of the old church embrace him. It felt like home, and he felt a little of his tension ease.

Skye Blackbird sat with her mother and stepfather in the third pew ahead of him. Her stepfather patted her on the back and smiled, then slid his other arm around his wife.

A lump thickened in Jake's throat. His own father

used to look at him with that same expression of pride. Lucky Skye. Jake wished he could roll back time and see that smile of joy on his own father's face again.

Enough of that maudlin musing. He glanced again at the Metis family. Skye seemed different here. Of course, she wasn't arguing, so that was an improvement. Jake's gaze lingered on her. She really was a beauty.

Her sleek black hair flowed over her shoulders, reaching nearly to her waist in a shining curtain. Her olive skin glowed with health. She wore a red dress in some loose and flowing material that made her look like an exotic bird.

But it wasn't her physical beauty that intrigued him. Her passion for what she believed in was mesmerizing. He was used to seeing it in his sisters, but the other women he'd come in contact with weren't lit from the inside in that fashion.

His gaze kept straying to the pew ahead of him until the service ended. Jake excused himself from his family and moved toward the Metis family. The Ojibwa family walked down the aisle toward him, and he stepped out to meet them. "Good morning, Skye, Mrs. Metis." He thrust out his hand to the man behind Mary. "We haven't met, but I'm Jake Baxter."

"Peter Metis." The other man took his hand in a vigorous grip. His dark eyes looked Jake over and seemed to find him worthy. His smile warmed Jake the same way his own father's had done. "You're going to put us on the map, I hear. I was initially opposed to your dig,

41

but it looks like I was wrong."

"This site will be famous," Jake agreed. He turned to Skye's mother. "Thanks for letting me dig, Mrs. Metis. You've done science a great service. This discovery will rock the world."

Mrs. Metis smiled. "I hope so, Jake," she said softly.

Skye stood quietly behind her mother. The two women looked much alike, and Jake could see Skye would age well. Mrs. Metis looked more like an older sister than her mother.

"I haven't seen any media around yet," Skye said. "Thank you for that."

"It won't last," he warned. "They'll get wind of it pretty soon."

"I know." She sounded resigned. "We might have to shut down the mine."

"It's for the best," Peter said, his expression soft. He patted her shoulder.

Skye bit her lip. She didn't look happy about it, and Jake told himself it wasn't his fault. He thrust his hands in his pockets and moved uneasily. "Would you all care to come out to the site and see what I've found?"

"I'm eager to see it," Peter said, his hand on his wife's back. "But we've got lunch plans today. We'll stop out and look it over soon."

"Are you calling the discovery anything special?" Skye asked.

"I hadn't thought that far ahead," Jake told her. "Maybe the Turtle Mountain site?"

Her dark eyes met his. "I was thinking maybe the

Blackbird site, named after my father."

Mrs. Metis clapped her hands. "That's a wonderful idea, Skye." She turned to Jake with an eager look. "Would that be all right?"

"Sure." He watched Skye's face light up. She must have really loved her father. Wonder what made a man tick that he could leave a beautiful wife and daughter? Another woman, maybe? Or wanderlust of some sort, though he should have kept in touch.

Jake bid the Metis family goodbye and followed his grandmother outside.

"Dinner should be ready," Gram said, taking Jake's arm.

His tension eased at his grandmother's touch. She'd been a rock for him and his sisters since the loss of their parents.

He patted her wrinkled hand. "I think I'll just grab something here in town and head out to the site," Jake said, ignoring the cries of disappointment from his sisters.

He saw a familiar blue truck drive past. Cameron Reynolds. Luckily, the other paleontologist hadn't come back to Jake's site, but it was only a matter of time before Cameron stumbled on what Jake was doing.

He kissed his sisters and grandmother goodbye and went to his SUV. He stopped for a burger at the local greasy spoon, then drove along the dirt road out to the mine.

He found his thoughts drifting to Skye Blackbird. She

intrigued him, and he wasn't sure he liked it. He made it a point to steer clear of women. A new dig rarely left time for dating, and he hated the way other men put a rush on a woman for a few months then walked away with hurt in their wake. Better to be lonely than to hurt someone.

He parked and walked up to the site. As he rounded the curve in the trail to the site, he thought he heard something. A sliding noise off to his left. He paused then continued. The path sheared away to his right, a steep drop that made him dizzy to look over.

Something caught at his ankles, and he stumbled. Throwing out a hand to catch himself, he encountered nothing but empty air. His arms flailed, and he tried to wrench his body toward the rock face and away from the cliff's edge, but he was too off balance.

He pinwheeled at the top of the cliff then pitched over the edge.

Feetfirst, he hurtled down the slope. He tried desperately to grasp tree roots as he shot past them, but his reaching fingers slid off. He tore a fingernail loose before slamming into a pine tree about halfway down. Spread-eagled along the steep cliff, he grabbed hold of the rock and tossed one leg over an outcropping. His slide down the mountain's face stopped, and he lay among the rocky rubble trying to catch his breath.

The sheer rock face rose above him. The steepness of it looked impossible to climb. How was he going to get up there? He peered around the tree that had stopped his plummet to destruction. The way was even steeper and more impossible down. His arms ached from hanging on to the rock.

The family wouldn't come looking for him for hours. They'd think he just got caught up in his work and was spending the night as usual. He was going to have to figure this one out on his own.

Tightening his grip, he worked his legs around so his feet were braced against the tree. The trunk seemed fragile and too weak to hold him for long, and he feared his weight would tear the roots from the shallow soil.

His body hurt from a dozen shallow cuts and bruises. Dust coated his tongue and lodged in his eyes. He was in a world of hurt, and his prospects weren't looking good.

Gritting his teeth against the pain, he glanced around for a finger- or toehold. There, just above his head, he spied a cupped rock he might be able to get his fingers around. He reached out and grasped it with throbbing fingers, then shoved himself up using his feet to push against the tree trunk.

The trunk tore lose just as his knee found a small indentation to fit into. Jake had never felt so vulnerable as he lay in the hot afternoon sun with nothing substantial to hang on to. Panting, he threw out his left hand and found a small root poking through the soil. Slowly and laboriously, he inched his way up the slope. Several times, his fingers missed their hold and he slid back down a few inches.

Finally, he reached the path at the top. With a final, monumental effort, he reached out and found a finger-hold then pulled himself onto the level path. His face pressed into the shallow dust-covered path, and he lay almost too exhausted to move.

He'd thought he was a dead man. Rolling to his back, he pulled in a few deep breaths. He licked dry lips and reached for his canteen, now that he had a free hand. The metallic taste washed the dust from his tongue, and he swished the refreshing water around in his mouth before spitting it out. Another deep swallow brought relief to his tight throat.

He got to his hands and knees and shook his head to clear it. His attention was caught by something along the path. He peered closer. Was that a wire? Touching it, he ran his fingers along it until he saw where it had been attached on each end to sticks pounded into the ground.

The wire stretched across the path in front of him, put there deliberately to make him trip. At first he couldn't believe it. Someone had tried to kill him. It made no sense.

Then it made perfect sense. Cameron Reynolds. If Jake were dead, Cameron could easily move in and take credit for the find, since it hadn't been announced yet. Cameron must not have realized Wynne had been working closely with him.

He was going to have to break his promise to Skye and put out a press release. It was the only way to stop Cameron.

His racing thoughts stopped. Skye. Could she have done this to try get rid of him? He didn't want to believe that, but he couldn't dismiss the notion.

Once on his feet, his vision swam and he shook his head to clear it. He needed help. His hand went to his pocket, but his cell phone was gone, lost in his slide down the mountain. The sheriff needed to be brought in on this, so he was going to have to drive to town to get him.

He hesitated. What if the wire was gone by the time he got back? He shrugged. It was a chance he'd have to take.

Walking like an old man, he turned and went back to his SUV. His vision kept blurring, and he found it hard to keep the SUV on his own side of the road. Another vehicle stopped in front of him, and he slammed on the brakes. His head snapped forward, then back and he sank into darkness.

The dusty SUV had almost T-boned her. Shaken, Skye gripped the steering wheel and tried to quiet the sudden thumping of her heart. Whoever he was, he'd run a stop sign and hit a rock. She threw open her door and hopped out onto the macadam road. Steam was escaping from the SUV's hood. As she neared the vehicle, she recognized the man inside.

Jake's head lolled to one side, and he was covered in blood and dirt. Skye ran forward and opened the vehicle's door. "Jake!" She touched his face, but he didn't respond. Her cell phone was in the truck.

Racing back to her truck, she scrabbled for her purse and found her cell phone. She dialed 911 and told the dispatcher to send an ambulance. Her father had always insisted on a first-aid pack in the truck, but Skye had never had occasion to use it. She opened the glove box and rummaged inside. She found antiseptic wipes, antibiotic ointment and Band-Aids.

Jake was moving restlessly by the time she got back to his SUV. His eyes fluttered, and he moaned when she cleansed his wounds with the wipes.

He sat up. "What happened?"

"You tell me. I found you passed out cold after you nearly hit me." Skye dabbed ointment on the cuts around his eyes and forehead. His lips were cracked, too, but she didn't think he'd take kindly to greasy ointment on them.

"Someone tried to kill me." He leaned forward onto the steering wheel. "I think I'm going to throw up."

Skye massaged the back of his neck. "Take deep breaths," she advised. She didn't like his pallor under the dirt. Trying not to hurt him, she probed his thick hair for lumps. She suspected he had at least a mild concussion.

"Ouch!" He jerked his head away. "I'm fine, quit fussing."

"You're not fine. And where's your hat?" she added, feeling like an idiot for asking the question. He didn't look the same without his hat. His vulnerability tugged at her heart, and she didn't like the way it made her feel.

"Fell off when I pitched over the cliff," he mumbled. He closed his eyes and leaned his head back against the headrest.

He'd fallen over a cliff? What if he had broken something? She touched his forehead, and his skin felt clammy. "Hang in there, Jake. Help is on the way."

"Should have run when I took one look at you," he mumbled. "So beautiful."

Her heart took a sudden leap like a deer running from a bear. He thought she was beautiful? She swallowed hard and stepped back as she heard the *wah-wah* of the ambulance in the distance.

Jake's eyes snapped open, and he stared at her. Skye was drawn into the dark depths. What made him tick? He seemed so driven about his career, so passionate.

He reached out his hand and touched her long braid with grimy fingers. "You tied your hair all up again. I liked it down." He closed his eyes again.

She would have sworn he wouldn't notice her hair in church. She didn't understand this attraction she felt toward him. He was a roving sort of guy, and she craved stability above all else. Men like him could chew her up and spit her out faster than she could react.

The ambulance's siren grew louder, and she turned to see the plume of dust behind the vehicle as it came toward them. The paramedics jumped from the ambulance and ran to Jake's SUV.

Jake opened his eyes again and sat up, waving them away. "I'm fine, just fine," he mumbled.

The paramedics ignored him, put a collar on his neck and proceeded to check his vitals. Once they were finished with the preliminaries, they started to

49

load him in the ambulance, but Jake balked.

"I'm not going," he said, his jaw thrust out.

"You'll have to sign a release," the older paramedic said.

"Fine, bring it on." Jake scribbled his name on the release, then ripped off the collar and handed it to them. "Call the sheriff. Someone rigged a wire across the path so I'd fall down the cliff," he told them.

"I'll call him right now." The paramedics walked toward the ambulance.

Skye looked him over again. He must have hit his head really hard. "Who would do such a thing? No one here would hurt you."

Jake's gaze focused on her. "You tell me. At first, I thought a rival might be at fault. But you have just as much motive."

"You can't be serious."

"You've been opposed to my presence right from the start. Whether you're the culprit or someone else, I have to move now. I don't scare easy. The only way to keep my discovery safe now is to announce it to the media."

"You can't do that!" She caught at his arm. "You have to know I don't want you dead!" Skye's voice trembled, and she bit her lip. The thought of Jake lying broken at the bottom of the cliff was a mental image that made her shudder.

Jake rubbed his forehead.

"Stop, you're making it bleed again." She grabbed his hand and pulled it away. "Jake, I wouldn't do something like that. I'll tell you to your face how I feel, but I won't be a sneak and a saboteur."

For the first time, he looked uncertain. "Maybe you're right." He shook his head, and his eyes thinned again as he stared into her face.

"You still don't look like you believe me."

"I don't know what to believe."

Skye hugged herself tightly. "Can you hire someone to guard the site?"

"You almost sound like you care."

"I care that someone might get hurt on our property."

"Ah, you're worried about lawsuits." His voice was ironic. "I signed a release not to hold your mother responsible, so it's not your problem."

But it was her problem. She chewed on her bottom lip. "I wish you'd come back to the shop with me. I'll give you some herbs to help with the healing and the muscle soreness."

He grinned. "Not a chance. You might finish the job with poison."

"You know better than that. You're just trying to be difficult." She wanted to cry, to put her head down and sob. It was the reaction to the near accident, she knew, but knowing that didn't make it easier to keep her voice from shaking.

This island had always seemed a safe haven for her. To realize someone wanted Jake dead made her glance toward the dark woods and wonder if someone was watching them. She'd never felt so exposed, so vulnerable. Who would do this?

"Don't look so scared." Jake took her hand. "I'll come with you."

His sudden capitulation drew her gaze from the shadowy forest. "Really?"

"I'm going to need all the help I can get to be back on the job tomorrow." He sounded grim, and the humor in his eyes faded.

"I'll help you to my truck," she said.

"I can walk by myself."

"At least you're smart enough to know you shouldn't be driving."

He got out of his SUV, and Skye slid behind the wheel and guided the SUV off the road.

"I'll have Max and Becca come get my vehicle later," Jake told her when she joined him beside her truck.

Skye nodded and went to the ambulance to tell them to have the sheriff meet them at her shop.

Jake opened the truck door and slid inside. "Where'd you get this beauty?"

Skye warmed to his praise of her "baby." Not many people appreciated the classic truck. "It was my father's." She felt, rather than saw, Jake's long glance in her direction.

"Your father's desertion really affected you."

Her heart gave a twinge at the compassion in his voice. "Yeah," she said. There were depths to Jake Baxter she found she liked.

"Did your mother ever try to find him?"

Skye nodded. "She hired a private investigator, but the trail petered out in Detroit."

"Had they been fighting?"

She nodded. "But no one thought he would just leave like that. Least of all me. We'd always been close."

Skye heard the raw emotion in her voice and changed the subject. "Any other ideas who could have put that wire up?"

"Besides you, you mean?" He grinned and held up his hands in a defensive posture. "Just kidding. Actually, I'm wondering if it was Cameron Reynolds."

"Why would you suspect him? Mother said he was charming."

"He's the sludge at the bottom of the pond. He lives and breathes for intrigue and deception. We used to be partners until he backstabbed me one too many times. He can't be trusted."

Skye felt the burden lighten. She'd rather believe it was an outsider, then she didn't have to worry about her friends and neighbors anymore. The sheriff would arrest this Cameron and life would resume as normal. "Are you going to tell the sheriff to check him out?"

"I might steer him in that direction." Jake looked grim.

They arrived at The Sleeping Turtle. Inside, she found the herbs she needed. "The white willow bark is especially good for pain and inflammation," she told him.

He accepted them with a skeptical grin. "Sounds like quackery to me, but I'll try them."

"I think you'll be pleasantly surprised," she said. "They work with the body and not against it like so many drugs. Natural is always better." She measured

53

out a dose and had him take it with a swig of water. "You're on your way to good health."

The bell at the front door jingled, and Sheriff Andrew Mitchell stepped into the store. Around fifty, his khaki pants were cinched up over a beer belly. "You look like something the Windigo chewed up and spit back," he said.

Jake grimaced. "I feel like it, too. It's got mighty sharp teeth." He told the sheriff what happened.

"You up to showing me where this is?" Sheriff Mitchell asked.

"After our local medicine woman's ministrations, I'm ready to take on the world," Jake said.

He winked at Skye, and she felt the heat of a blush move up her neck to her cheeks.

"Hey, don't be making fun of Skye. She's helped more people than you can count." Sheriff Mitchell followed them to the outside. "We might as well all go in my car." He opened the door for them, and they got in the back.

Once they reached the mine, Jake led them up the slope toward the dig. He moved slowly and winced several times. Skye frowned as she watched him. It would be useless to say anything. He'd never admit to the pain he was feeling.

"Right here," Jake said. "You can see where I went over the edge."

"Hmm." The sheriff knelt and looked at the path. "I don't see anything but this stick."

"What?" Jake scanned the path.

Skye knelt and looked around with him. The rocky path was free of obstruction other than the stick the sheriff indicated. No wires that she could see.

"You sure you didn't stumble over a stick?"

Jake's voice rose, and he stood with his fists on his hips. "Sheriff, it was right here. A wire tied to a stick on either side. Look, here are the holes where the sticks were."

"Could be snake holes," the sheriff said.

Skye could tell the sheriff didn't believe Jake. She wasn't sure she did, either. Maybe it was a way to get her to agree to announce the discovery of the dinosaur nursery.

Chapter Four

The patter of rain on the tent awakened Jake. The cold ground intensified the ache he felt clear to his bones. So much for Skye's herbal remedies. He sat up and laboriously crawled out of his sleeping bag. His family had begged him to sleep at Windigo Manor last night, but he'd been adamant about protecting the eggs he'd found.

He was going to have to get help, and Skye wouldn't like what he had to do to get it.

He wished there was some other way, but this discovery was too important to risk losing. He splashed cold water on his face and downed the herbs Skye had given him. They'd helped last night, though he doubted they'd touch the pain he was feeling this morning.

Max had retrieved Jake's hat and cell phone from the bottom of the cliff. The hat was now even more decrepit-looking. Jake clapped the hat over his unruly hair and threw back the flap on the tent.

The cold drizzle depressed his spirits even further. He peered at the gloomy sky and shook his head. Trudging through the mud, he checked his site and found everything as it had been left last night.

"How are you feeling today?"

He turned to see Skye standing on the path with a plate of food in her hand.

"Sore." His stomach rumbled at the aroma of sausage. "I hope that food is for me."

"I'm not the best cook in the world, but at least it's hot. I hope you like biscuits and gravy. I wanted to see how you're feeling." She hesitated, then went on. "I hope you've gotten over your suspicion of me. I wouldn't do anything to hurt you."

He searched her face. "Are you trying to bribe me?"

Her lips lifted in a smile. "Would it work?"

"Sorry, but no. I'm going to have to call the media today."

She sighed. "That's what I thought. But you can still have the breakfast."

Jake grabbed a camp chair for her and one for himself, and accepted the plate of food. He tucked into his meal with gusto and downed it in three minutes. "I was starved," he said. "I don't think I had dinner last night."

She cocked her head to one side. "You look better this

56

morning—not so green around the gills."

He realized with a sense of shock that his pain had lessened since taking her remedies. "I'm actually feeling better. Those herbs must have worked." Either that or it was being around her. He liked to watch the way her eyes grew mysterious. The bone structure in her face intrigued him with its sharp planes and angles. She didn't need makeup.

He heard a vehicle pull into the parking lot below them and looked down. "Great, just great," he muttered when he saw Cameron's vehicle. "I'd better head him off at the pass."

"I'll come with you. I need to get back to town." Skye grabbed the empty plate of food and followed Jake down the steep path.

They met Cameron about halfway up. Jake barred the other man's way to the dig. "What are you doing here again, Reynolds?"

"I thought I'd see how you were doing. I heard you had a spill yesterday."

"Oh, you heard, did you? And I suppose you had nothing to do with it." Jake watched his former partner's face for signs of guilt, but the man's smile didn't diminish. Jake knew Cameron was a practiced liar.

"You're jumping at shadows," Cameron said smoothly. "I heard it was an accident. Are you saying someone pushed you?"

"I'm saying someone stretched a wire across the path in the worst possible spot so I'd go plummeting down

57

the hill. I asked myself who would do such a despicable thing. Your name came to mind."

"I think you watch too many murder mysteries." Cameron's gaze traveled to Skye. "You have to be Skye Blackbird. You look just like your beautiful mother."

Skye smiled, and Jake wanted to snarl at the bedazzled expression on her face. Cameron's charm had done its work, even on her.

Cameron took her hand and held on to it a moment too long. Skye finally pulled it away, but there was a flush to her cheeks Jake didn't like. He told himself he wasn't jealous.

"My mother says you're a paleontologist, too." she said.

"If you want to call him that," Jake muttered.

"What?" Skye finally turned her head and looked at him.

"Nothing," Jake said. "I need to get to town. If you want to find out what I'm doing, Reynolds, you'll have to wait and see it on the evening news."

For the first time the smooth expression on Cameron's face changed. "Wait, what are you talking about? You need my help."

"I don't need anything from you. Least of all that ever-present knife you're about to plunge into my back." Jake grabbed Cameron's arm and propelled him down the last of the path to the parking lot.

Cameron twisted, but couldn't slip out of Jake's grip. He'd always been a weakling, Jake thought with a curl

58

of his lip. Jake released him at the door to Cameron's fancy truck.

"After you, Reynolds."

Cameron gave him a furious look, but flung himself into the driver's seat. He floored the engine and spun gravel from his tires as he took off.

"You didn't have to be so rude," Skye said.

"Don't be suckered by his good looks. He'll chew you up and spit you out before you can blink."

"I'm not that naive," she said with a trace of haughtiness.

"You could have fooled me. I saw the way you were ogling him."

"I have never ogled anyone in my life!" Her eyes sparked fire, and she put her hands on her hips. "I don't know why I bothered to bring you breakfast. Obviously, the slide down the mountain failed to teach you anything." She flounced to her pickup and sped away.

Jake gritted his teeth and got in his SUV. It was just as well they were on the outs. She was too attractive for his peace of mind.

Skye fumed as she raced the truck toward town. He'd taken her peace offering and flung it back in her face. Ogled indeed. Heat burned her cheeks. Maybe she'd been a little tongue-tied at Cameron's appearance, but the man looked and acted like some kind of movie star. Someone like him had never appeared in Turtle Town before. She guessed she'd been a little starstruck.

He wasn't your typical paleontologist. Could he have

stretched the wire across the path? Or had that even happened? She didn't know what to believe.

Cameron's truck was parked in front of The Sleeping Turtle when she arrived. Her heart beat a little faster as she got out and went inside. Maybe he wasn't in her store at all, but in the coffee shop next door.

As she neared the door, she heard her mother's laughter and Cameron's deep answering chuckle. Warmth traveled up her neck to her cheeks, and she smoothed the wisps of hair that had pulled loose from her braid. The fact that Jake highly disapproved of Cameron only made it more pleasant to defy the pale-ontologist who was such a thorn in her flesh.

She went inside. "I'm back," she called.

"We have a special guest," her mother called. "Have you two met?"

"I had the pleasure of meeting your lovely daughter a little while ago."

Cameron's smile was as bright as the noonday sun, and Skye almost had to close her eyes against the bril-liance. The man's charm was incredible. He'd missed his calling by choosing science over the silver screen.

"I can see where she gets her beauty," he said, turning back to Mary.

Skye's mother simpered. That was the only word for it, Skye thought incredulously. In that moment, her bedazzlement with Cameron snapped. Had the same silly expression been on her face when they met at the mine? If so, no wonder Jake had been so contemp-tuous.

"I thought I'd look for something for my mother for her birthday," Cameron said. He turned to look at the display of herbal candles on an endcap.

Did someone like him even have a mother? Skye could imagine him emerging fully grown from a magical spring like a young Adonis. "We have the candles and some wonderful aromatherapy products down the next aisle," she told him.

"Mom might like the aromatherapy. Would you mind showing me?"

Conscious of the way her mother was looking on with approval, Skye led him to the display. "Do you know if she has a favorite scent? The lavender ones are particularly popular with the older ladies."

"She loves lilacs, so that might be a good choice if you have it."

She started to leave him to peruse the products, when he stopped her with his hand on her arm.

"I was wondering if you were in full agreement with what Baxter is doing at the mine site?" he asked.

"I don't have much say in it," she said shortly. "My mother owns the mine and the land around it."

"Yes, but I was under the impression you were the manager."

"I am, but it's Mother's property. If she had asked me, I wouldn't have given permission for you to dig."

He leaned toward her and turned his smile on full wattage, but this time Skye merely blinked at the brilliance.

"What he's planning will harm your mining operation. We have to delay his announcement. Once the world hears what he's found, this town will be crawling with geologists and paleontologists from around the world."

"How do you know what he's found?"

His smile faltered. "I suspect it's a dinosaur nursery. Hundreds of eggs. Few sites like it have been found."

Skye was careful to let her expression betray nothing. "What makes you think that?"

"I saw some shapes that looked—shall we say, intriguing—the first day I was at the site. I'm a good scientist. I recognized the site's possibilities as quickly as Jake did."

She didn't bother to hide her skepticism. "Why would you want to help me stop the announcement?"

"I like you and your mother. I'd hate to see you taken advantage of by the likes of Jake Baxter."

"Forgive me if I don't believe you. You don't even know us." She was suddenly weary of the whole conversation. People using other people, each playing one against the other in sneaky ways. She wanted this man gone from her store and her life. Jake as well.

His smile faded. "Okay, I'll tell you the truth. Jake took credit for something I found. I want to get back at him, but I need your help."

"Funny, he says *you're* the one who betrayed him."

"Look up the Baxter find in Venezuela. You won't find a mention of my name, but I'm the one who called him in on that project."

He seemed sincere. Skye shrugged. "I don't know

how we'll stop it anyway. He went to town to call the media."

"We have to stop him!" He grabbed her hand and propelled her toward the door.

Skye wrenched away. "There's nothing I can do."

"Well, I can." He left her standing in the aisle and ran out the door.

Skye stared after him. She was tempted to call Jake and warn him. But what could Cameron do anyway? It was probably too late.

Maybe she'd just follow Cameron and see what he was going to do. She wouldn't want him to hurt Jake. Not that the big paleontologist couldn't take care of himself, but what if Jake's suspicions were correct and Cameron had put a wire out to trip him?

The Detroit newspaper was flying in some reporters in a few minutes. Other papers has sent theirs by ferry. Jake stood in his room at Windigo Manor and tried to decide what to wear.

"Wear that tie," Wynne said, pointing to a burgundy one. "And pair it with a navy blazer and khaki slacks."

"I don't want to dress up," he grumbled. "I think a clean shirt and jeans will do just fine. The newspapers like a little bit of color in their stories."

"Maybe you're right." Becca riffled through the clothes in the closet and pulled out a red denim shirt. "This looks good. And make sure you take your hat. I'll clean it up for you. The lady reporters will swoon over you."

"That's the last thing I need," Jake said. Before he could stop it, he had an image of Skye swooning into his arms. He hid a grin. She'd likely spit on his boots before she'd swoon.

"I'll be glad when this is all out in the open," Becca said. "It was too close for comfort yesterday."

Jake glanced at his watch. "It's almost show time. Let's get out in the yard."

The rain had ended, and the sun's warmth left little dampness in the ground. Jake settled on the porch to await the helicopter. Ten minutes later the sound of the rotors roused him from a near doze. He stood and went to greet the reporters just as a car bearing the rest pulled up.

Once they were set up, he stepped into place. "I've called you here to announce something of great significance to the scientific community. And not just to scientists but to the whole world. How many of you are familiar with the dinosaur nests found in Mongolia?"

"I am." An older man of about sixty waved his hand. "Are you saying that's what you've found?"

"Exactly," Jake said.

"Hold on a minute." Cameron Reynolds stepped out from behind the side of the house. "This is a hoax."

"Who are you?" the reporter asked.

"Cameron Reynolds."

"I've heard of you. You discovered that big T-Rex last year."

Jake gritted his teeth and forced himself not to object. It would make him look like a fool. "If you'd like to follow me out to the site, I can show you," he said.

He was aware of Cameron's smug smile as Jake rounded up the reporters into his SUV. Cameron followed in his truck. What did he have up his sleeve? Jake didn't trust him, but there was little he could do about it in front of the reporters.

The reporters and their photographers trooped up the path to the site. Jake stepped to the dig and looked down. The dig was exactly as he left it with his tools spread out and the land exposed.

With one exception. His eggs were gone.

Rage built in his chest, and he whirled to find the other paleontologist. Cameron's smile was smug and then his eyes widened when he saw Jake leap.

Jake tackled him and bore Cameron to the ground. "What did you do with my eggs?" he shouted.

"There were never eggs here," Cameron panted, trying to break Jake's hold on him.

The reporters were milling around and shouting questions. Jake was barely aware of them until one of them grabbed his arm and tried to pull him off Cameron. Jake wanted to pummel the paleontologist into the ground, but he realized how it looked to the reporters.

He forced himself to release Cameron and stand up. His blood pumped through his veins in a hard rush. He took a deep breath and told himself to calm down. He forced his hands to unclench. The reporters were staring at them with avid faces. He needed to regain control of the situation.

"Talk to my sister. She saw the eggs, too."

Just past the crowd of reporters, he saw Skye running up the path toward him. She reached the top, and her eyes widened as she took in the situation. "What's going on?"

"Lover boy here has stolen my eggs," Jake said bitterly.

Cameron got up and brushed the dirt from his slacks. "It's a plot he hatched with his sister to get publicity," he told the reporters.

"Look around you," Jake said. "See the egg shapes in the rocks? They're dinosaur eggs embedded in the stones."

"Just looks like round rocks to me," the head reporter responded. "I think we're going to have more proof than this to run a story."

"There were eggs here," Skye said.

Jake whipped his head around to look at her and saw Cameron do the same. Why would she help? It was to her benefit to keep this under wraps for a while.

"I saw them," she said.

"Who are you?" the older reporter asked.

"Skye Blackbird, the manager of the mine here. Someone has tampered with the evidence." Her gaze was on Cameron, and he flushed but said nothing.

The reporter shook his head. "There isn't much to go on here." He glanced around at the site. "Call us again when you have more proof."

"I'll get you proof," Jake said tightly. "I have some experts I can call to help me excavate more eggs. And next time I'll call people who won't be misled by a saboteur." He gave Cameron a long look.

He stomped down the path to the SUV. He should have stayed to thank Skye but he was thinking only of setting things right. Once he accompanied the ferry riders' car back to town, he'd find his eggs. But first he'd make a call to Kimball Washington. Kimball had been his mentor for many years. He'd know what to do.

Chapter Five

Skye had been as shocked to hear herself speak up to the reporters as Jake had been, but the thought of the slimy Cameron Reynolds getting away with his ploy was enough to make her speak before she thought. At least the media wouldn't be descending just yet.

She watched the vehicles disappear around the bend in a cloud of dust then went inside the mine. The workers had left for the day, and the place was eerily quiet. She'd told her mother she'd be late and what she was going to do. Though her mother had said nothing, she knew she thought it was time to put the past away, too.

She could hear the drip of water from somewhere. The dank smell of earth followed her down the corridor to her office. Skye's office often felt like a haven to her.

Here she could see the things her father had left behind. She could open his humidor and sniff the last faint scent of his Cuban cigars, though they were stale by now. Still, it seemed he could walk in the door at any moment. She liked it best when the mine was empty, and she could close her eyes and go back eight years in time. Silly, she knew. It was time she grew up.

She sat at the battered metal desk and put her head in her hands. Events seemed to be spiraling out of her control. This old garnet mine had served its purpose of getting her past the grief of her father's abandonment. She was twenty-four now, a grown woman. It was time she left childish things behind.

It was time to pack up all her father's possessions. The thought made her feel as though she were having a panic attack, even though she'd come here intending to pack. Skye took a few deep breaths. *In and out, in and out.* Once the constriction eased in her chest, she found a box from the closet and opened the drawers.

She began to pack away the things, forcing herself not to linger over each one. It wasn't as though she were throwing them away. She could still take them from her closet at home and look at them if she felt the need.

Once the desk was clean, she put the box under her arm and went down the corridor toward the exit. Halfway there, she glanced to the left corridor where the Mitchell tube was located. If only Peter would agree to helping them shore it up and search there.

She set the box on the floor and stepped into the branching corridor. The floor was uneven and damp. Rock crumbled from the sides. She knew it was unsafe, but she had a hunch about this tube. She walked along the narrowing tunnel as far as she could, though she began to feel claustrophobic as the ceiling lowered and the walls grew narrower. She heard a sound and froze. "Hello?" There was nothing to be frightened of. It was likely a worker who had forgotten something, or maybe even James.

"Pop? Are you there?" When there was no answer, she began to move again. She touched the dank walls at the dead end. Time to go back. Her dream was as boxed off as the end of this tunnel where the last rockfall had taken place two years ago.

As she reached the main corridor, she heard another sound and started to turn. Something hit her out of nowhere. She saw a bright flash of stars, then darkness claimed her.

Jake bade farewell to the reporters then drove back out to the mine. He glowered at Cameron as he passed the other man in town. Cameron smiled back, a smirk that made Jake want to stop his SUV and pounce on him again. But he set his lips in a firm line and drove on. Cameron would lose the battle.

Once in the parking lot of the Turtle Mine, he grabbed his cell phone and fished out his address book from his satchel in the tent. Kimball Washington should be done with classes by now. He punched in the number and pressed Send.

Kimball's gravelly voice answered. "Washington here."

"Hey, Kimball, it's Jake Baxter."

"Jake! What are you up to these days? Great work you did on your last dig. I've been looking over your notes."

"I have something even more important I need you to help me with."

The African-American professor of paleontology had been Jake's mentor ever since he took Kimball's class his freshmen year at the University of Chicago. Jake relied on him in more ways than he could count. He explained the problem, and Kimball promised to come up to the island and have a look.

Jake clicked off his phone with a decisive punch of his index finger. *Take that, Cameron Reynolds.* The media wouldn't be able to ignore his find once the highly respected Kimball Washington had his say.

If he could just find his missing eggs.

Jake scowled again at the thought of Cameron's perfidy. Those eggs were priceless. Where could he have stashed them?

He went to his SUV, smiling as he noticed Skye's truck. She was always so carefully put together, it seemed strange to think of her driving that dilapidated vehicle. She was a bundle of contradictions. Just like today when she'd jumped to his defense in spite of her own opposition to having the dig expanded.

He should thank her.

Jake paused at the door to his SUV, then shrugged and went to the mine entrance. The doorknob turned easily. She really should keep it locked when she was in there alone. While crime wasn't a major problem on the island, she was a young, beautiful woman alone in a remote place.

He stepped into the mine. Lights had been strung up along the corridor, but the illumination didn't push the gloom back very far. His throat closed. He didn't like it here. It was too close, too tight.

He'd gotten lost in some caves when he was ten, and he still didn't like them. Luckily, most of his digs didn't involve caves. He'd get back under the stars once he did his duty. "Skye? Where are you?"

The steady drip of water nearby was the only sound in the shadowy corridor. It felt as if his nerves were on fire. Places like this made him clench his teeth and force himself not to run.

Beginning to sweat in spite of the dank cold inside the mine, he trod along the corridor to a place where it terminated in another hall. Another minute and he would bolt out of here.

The panic began to surge even more and he turned to leave. He almost didn't see the form on the floor in the dim light from the lone bulb above his head.

"Skye?" He knelt beside her and touched her face. His own panic eased as he looked her over. A trickle of blood ran from a cut on her head. The pulse in her neck beat strongly against his fingers. Good. He rolled her gently on her back and checked for any broken bones. His cell phone was in his pocket fortunately, and he pulled it out. No signal underground. He'd have to go outside to place the call.

Did he dare to leave her alone? "Skye," he said.

71

"Wake up." The canteen attached to his belt still held a bit of water. He unscrewed the cap and upended the container over Skye's face. Splatters of water hit her face. She murmured and moved her head from side to side. Then she sputtered, and her eyes opened.

"What'd you do that for?" She tried to sit up, batting his helping hands away. "I'm fine."

"At least you've still got your spunk," he said dryly. He slipped his arm around her back in spite of her protest. "What happened?"

The walls felt like they were closing in on him. He had to get her on her feet and get out of here. His heart pounded against his chest as though it would beat him out of the mine.

She groaned and held her head. "Someone hit me."

Jake caught his breath. "Did you see who it was?"

"No, it came from behind me." She looked at the canteen in his hand. "Any water left?"

"Here." He handed her the canteen, and she took a swig then grimaced. "Tastes like metal."

"That critical spirit is going to get you in trouble." He tried to smile, but the panic was building by the second.

Her lips turned up a bit. "Sorry, I didn't mean it. Thanks for the water." She handed him the canteen then groaned again when she tried to get up. "My head's killing me."

"We need to have a doctor look at you. You could have a concussion."

"I'm fine." But she didn't shrug his arm away when

he helped her to her feet. She swayed a bit then stood firmer.

He wished he could see better. "Are you feeling stronger?"

"I think so. My head still hurts though." She touched her head. "Feels like a goose egg up there."

"Let's get out where I can see it." He led her toward the door, but she stumbled. A light shone over head, so he made himself stop and probe her thick hair. "It's cut a little, too. We need to get you to town."

And get him out of this mine before he puked.

Skye shivered. "My mom will take care of me. Can you drive me?"

"That's a dumb question." He helped her outside, trying not to hurry her too much, though he wanted to bolt. The air never felt so good. Breathing in the fresh air greedily, he felt the tension ease from his shoulders.

He helped her to the SUV and got her into the passenger side, then got under the steering wheel. "Should I lock up the mine?"

She shook her head. "We never lock it."

"So anyone can come in and tamper with the machinery?"

She bit her lip. "I never thought about it like that. We don't even have a key for the place." She shrugged. "I don't guess it matters, since we're going to shut it down." Her face changed. "Oh, I forgot my box! Would you mind going back after it?"

He'd rather eat raw fish. He swallowed hard. "Where is it?"

"On the floor near where you found me."

His manhood wouldn't let him tell her he feared going back inside. Setting his jaw, he nodded. "Lock the doors while I'm gone." He didn't know if her attacker was still in the area, but he wasn't about to take any chances.

She nodded and punched the power button to lock all the doors. His mouth went dry as he started back toward the mine. He took a deep breath, ducked inside and dashed to the spot where he'd found Skye. He scooped up the box and ran back to the exit as if a wildcat were on his tail.

As he reached the door, he thought he heard something. Hesitating in the corridor, he started in that direction, then stopped. He couldn't make himself take another step. Besides, Skye needed medical attention, he told himself.

Relief made him feel light-headed as he went back outside into the falling twilight. He approached the SUV. Several steps from the vehicle, something zinged by his head and slammed into the driver's window. It shattered.

"Hit the floor!" he shouted to Skye. He dove to the ground and crawled forward.

Two more rocks zipped by him. He needed to get to the SUV and get them both out of danger. As he neared the vehicle, the door swung open and he looked into Skye's strained face where she lay on the seat.

"Get in!" She crawled back to her own side and slid to the floor.

He got to his hands and knees and dove in, then slammed the door behind him. The vehicle was already running. Crouching as low as he could, he tromped on the accelerator.

Only when they were a mile down the road did he breathe easier. He glanced at Skye as she crawled back into her seat. "Got any idea who might be lobbing rocks at us?"

Skye shuddered. "I can't imagine who it would be. Unless—" she broke off.

"Unless?" he prompted.

She hesitated again and pulled her long black braid over her shoulder, worrying it with her fingers. "There's a disgruntled customer who tried to shake me off the ladder last week."

"What? Did you call the sheriff?"

She shook her head. "I didn't want to get her in trouble. She's grieving her son. She came to the store for some herbs. When she explained what was wrong with him, I told her to take him to the doctor because I thought it might be appendicitis. She insisted on buying the herbs anyway. I guess she never took him and he died. She blames me for not giving her the right herbs now."

"That's crazy!"

"Yeah, well, Tallulah Levenger has always been a little different."

"Where does she live? Maybe if I go put a little fear in her she'll leave us alone."

Skye's eyes were shadowed. "She was probably just

deranged with grief when she came to the shop last week."

"So you think she trailed you to the mine, knocked you out, then lobbed rocks at you?" Skye was too soft and wanted to believe the best of people. He knew any person was capable of just about any action. It wouldn't be wise to discount the woman.

"It wouldn't hurt to have the sheriff check her out," he told her.

"I suppose." Skye rubbed her forehead.

"Your head still aching?"

"I don't suppose you have any of the willow bark with you, do you?"

"As a matter of fact, it's in my backpack." He pulled to the side of the road in order to reach behind the seat with one hand. He grabbed it, then tossed it in her lap.

She rummaged through it and found the herb and swallowed it. "That should help."

Jake suddenly realized he was feeling better himself. "You might have something there," he said. "My muscle aches are much better even though it has to have worn off by now. It must have fixed me."

"You sound surprised." Her lips curved into a smile.

"I am. I thought it was a lot of hokum."

"We all have prejudices to overcome," she said, a full-fledged grin breaking forth.

Jake made a noncommittal sound. He grabbed his cell phone. "I about forgot to call the sheriff. I'll have him meet us at your mom's."

"I hate all this." She sounded near tears. "It's sobering

76

to think someone hates me enough to want to attack me like that."

"Maybe I was the target and not you."

"Tallulah wouldn't have any beef with you," she reminded him.

"Maybe it wasn't Tallulah," he said, thinking of Cameron.

But she didn't hear him. Her head was back against the headrest, and her eyes were closed. She needed to be looked at. He dropped the SUV's gear into Drive and took off toward town again.

It felt like a woodpecker had taken up residence inside her skull. Skye suppressed a groan and opened her eyes. Her vision seemed blurry, and she blinked to try to clear it.

"Almost there," Jake said. He reached across the seat and touched her cheek.

The roughness of his fingers sharpened her senses, and almost without thinking, she leaned her face into the caress. His fingers stilled, then his thumb traced the curve of her cheek. The sweetness of the moment was almost more than she could bear. Who would have thought she and Jake Baxter would share some strange attraction between them?

Maybe she *was* concussed. She straightened up and pulled away. "Did you get the sheriff?"

"Yep. I told you, but you wouldn't wake up."

He turned the corner onto Houghton Street and stopped in front of her mother's house. A four-square brick home, it had been built at the turn of the century by one of the Welsh fishermen who'd immigrated to the United States and settled along Superior's shores. When this part of the island had been deeded to the Ojibwa tribe, her great-grandfather had taken possession of this property and everyone in town called it the Blackbird house.

Someday it would be hers.

But not for many years, she prayed. Jake opened his door and came around to assist her. She felt dizzy as she stood and leaned on his arm. He helped her to the house and pressed the doorbell.

The sensation of his muscular arm around her waist was more disconcerting than she would have liked. Skye held herself stiffly, afraid of the way her pulse raced and her mouth felt as dry as the arid Windigo spring.

Her mother opened the door. "Skye, what on earth?" She grabbed her daughter and helped her inside.

Peter came through the door from the garage. He hurried to help and swung Skye into his arms. She leaned her head against his chest. He'd been the best father he knew how to be. She shouldn't be comparing him to her own father so much. "I'm okay now," she said, smiling up at him.

"Good thing I just got here from the bank," he said. "I thought you were going to faint for a minute. What did you do to her?" he asked, looking at Jake.

"He saved me, that's what he did," she said. "Someone knocked me out at the mine. Then when we came out, someone tried to stone us."

Peter's eyes widened. His gaze darted to Jake again. "It appears I owe you my thanks. This girl is special to all of us." His eyes misted with tears. "We'd better call the sheriff."

"Jake already did." Skye eased to the sofa and leaned her head against the back. "Mother, could you take a look at the cut on my head and see if it needs a butterfly?"

"Don't you think we'd better call a doctor?" Jake's voice sounded worried.

"I shall tend to my own daughter." Her mother moved to Skye's side and began to probe her head.

Jake backed away. A knock came at the door. "That's probably the sheriff," he said.

"I'll let him in." Peter hurried to the door and ushered the sheriff to the living room.

Sheriff Mitchell frowned as he saw Skye. "What's going on out at that mine?"

"I wish we knew," Jake said, his mouth a grim line.

"Wait, where's the box?" Skye asked. When Jake brought it to her, she opened it and scanned the contents. "His eagle feather is gone!"

"Eagle feather?" Jake asked.

"It was his most prized possession," her mother said. "He won it in a Grass Dance. I never understood why he didn't take it with him."

"It's gone now," Skye said, closing the box. "It has to be Tallulah. She asked to buy it from me several times last year. She told me she wanted the power from it. She probably threw the stones to drive us off so we would leave the box." She told Mitchell about Tallulah's behavior since her son's death.

"Let's not jump to conclusions," the sheriff said. "I'll talk to her."

Skye nodded. "Just get my eagle feather back."

Chapter Six

Skye found her wariness around Jake lightening up, and the sensation was somewhat akin to being adrift on Superior in her father's old boat, now lying scuttled in the barn. The holes in her armor were not of her own making, and she managed to summon resentment toward him for that. He was in her thoughts often over the next few days, no matter how she tried to fill her time with making dreamcatchers.

"Skye, I'm running out of some of our herbs," her mother told her on Wednesday morning.

"I'll search for more," Skye said. Maybe a trek in the forest would keep her thoughts from wandering to the way Jake had tried to protect her from the assailant. She'd never had anyone show such sacrifice for her.

She took her canvas sack and drove out to Windigo forest, a vast tract with native trees that had never seen the lumberjack's axe. She parked along the side of the road and entered the woods.

This was her favorite part of her job. Secrets lay in the forest, meadows with herbs and roots that could help her people. The cool rush of shadow and the fecund scent of wildflowers and decaying leaves lifted her spirits.

She walked along a path her people had used for decades, then plunged through brush along a new trajectory, stopping to check her compass occasionally. By noon her bag was bulging with herbs and roots, and she felt cleansed, reborn by the forest.

She had turned to head back to the road when she heard the rhythmic chop-chop of an axe. She followed the sound. No one was supposed to chop wood in this forest.

Pushing past a tangle of forsythia, she stepped into a clearing and found a lean-to. Drying animal skins hung on a rack beside the structure, and a curl of smoke rose from a firepit that held a spit with a rabbit cooking over the low flame.

She should probably leave. Whoever was living here was doing so illegally and might not take kindly to being discovered. She could tell the park ranger to check it out. The chopping had stopped, and only the drone of insects disturbed the quiet of the deep woods.

A frisson of panic assailed her for no real reason, and the hair on the back of her neck stood up. Skye winced as her retreating footsteps crunched dead leaves.

A form materialized from the shadows in front of her. "I know you," the man said.

Skye nearly screamed. She took a step back. "Wilson, you scared me. What are you doing out here?" She felt almost giddy with relief.

"I live here."

She hadn't seen Wilson New Moon in nearly two months, she realized. The forty-year-old mentally challenged man often stopped by her shop to talk about his hobby of balsam airplanes. She sold them in her shop, and he eked out an existence on the income.

"I wondered why you hadn't been in the shop lately. I have some money for you," she told him.

Wilson scratched insect bites that reddened his balding pate, then hitched up his baggy jeans. He looked like he'd lost weight. Skye frowned as her gaze took in his filthy plaid flannel shirt. She'd never seen him look so unkempt.

He blinked. "Be careful, Skye. She hates you."

"Who hates me?" Skye wondered if she could coax him out of the woods and into town, where Dr. Bobber could take a look at him.

"Her." Wilson shuddered. "I seen her watching you."

"Wilson, have you been eating?" Skye didn't like the feverish look in his eyes or the gray pallor of his skin.

He nodded. "Want some rabbit?"

"Why are you out here?"

He glanced around in a furtive way that made Skye's mouth go dry. "She told me to come out here."

"Who is she?"

"Asibikaashi. The Spider Woman." Tears sprang to his eyes and trickled down his face, leaving dirty tracks in their wake.

Skye was growing more alarmed by Wilson's manner. "You know there's no such thing as Asi-

82

bikaashi. Jesus has saved us from the old superstitions."

She couldn't figure out why he was so frightened. The old Ojibwa legend of Asibikaashi was that of a kindly spider who wove a web to help the sun find all the dispersed Ojibwa people. Her people loved and revered the legend.

Wilson had accepted Christ in church about six months ago, and she didn't understand why he'd slipped back into some of his old beliefs.

He shook his head mournfully. "I'd thought so, too, Skye, then she came. I was in my tent, and she whispered to me and told me what had to be done. I wish Jesus would kill her." More tears slipped down his face. He looked into the woods. "You have to get out of here."

Skye would like nothing better than to get out of here. Adrenaline still made her feel jittery. "Come with me, Wilson," she urged. "We can get your money."

He shook his head. "She'll find me if I leave." He backed away, then turned and plunged through the woods.

Skye called after him, but he jumped a stream and disappeared from view. She thought about going after him but knew it was useless. Wilson was the most woods-savvy person she knew. If he didn't want to be found, it would be like trying to catch the smoke rising from the cooking rabbit.

As she made her way out of the forest, she puzzled over Wilson's cryptic comments. She was tempted to dismiss his warning as the fabrications of Wilson's childish mind, but remembering the sound of rocks slamming into Jake's SUV convinced her there might be something to Wilson's ramblings.

Maybe she should talk to the sheriff about it. And Jake. He could help her figure out what was going on. Skye realized she had more faith in his ability than in the sheriff's. Jake was a real man in every sense of the word, and his strength drew her. She knew she had no chance of attracting him. He'd seen beautiful women from every far-flung corner of the globe.

She smiled wryly as she reached the road and got back into her truck. Of course, she was as helpless to stay out of Jake's path as a fly buzzing furiously to get out of a web. Jake could be just as deadly to her future happiness, too.

Jake pulled his damp shirt away from his chest and wiped the perspiration from his forehead with the back of his arm. He'd succeeded in excavating another clutch of eggs, and the round shapes lying before him were worth every drop of sweat. Kimball Washington would be impressed when he arrived tomorrow.

Jake glanced at his watch. Nearly two o'clock. He had a good five hours of daylight left to work. The soreness in his muscles had disappeared, and he felt good today, relishing the hard work at the dig.

Wynne stood and stretched her back. "I'm ready for some water. Want a bottle?"

"Sure." He watched her go to the cooler. "I appreciate your helping me this summer, Wynne. I know you turned down a pretty attractive project."

She smiled as she handed him the water. "How did you hear about that?"

"Becca told me."

"She's a blabbermouth." She uncapped her water and took a swig.

"I know, but if you want to accept it and go, I'll understand."

"No, you wouldn't. You think digging up eggs is the most important job in the world." She grinned and poked him in the stomach. "And I'm enjoying being with my big brother. We don't get time like this very often. Besides, you need my help."

"True. I don't know what I would have done without you these past couple of weeks. I'll be able to get some funding to finish out the dig once it's announced, though. And if you want to go then, I won't yell."

"Becca would." Wynne sat on a rock and wiped her forehead. "But seriously, Jake, I'm enjoying it."

A sound caught his attention and he looked around to see a truck pull into the parking lot below them. "Skye's here." The lightness he felt when he saw her truck surprised him.

"I think you're a goner, Jake," Wynne said, her gaze lingering on his face. "Your roving days are about over."

He shook his head. "She's just a friend."

"Go ahead and deceive yourself a little longer," Wynne said. "I've never seen that look in your eyes before. I hope you'll like living on Windigo Island.

Skye will never leave here."

"You're nuts. I have no intention of staying here the rest of my life."

"I don't know, this dig might take years to fully excavate. By then, your wanderlust might be gone."

Jake knew himself well enough to know he'd always be drawn to new discoveries, new horizons. Though this dig was exciting, there were more sites out there waiting to be uncovered.

He shook his head. "You're wrong, Wynne. I'm never getting married."

Wynne raised an eyebrow. "Never say never, big brother."

Her certainty irked him, and he felt his temper rising as he saw Skye coming up the path to the dig. He'd show Wynne she was wrong.

Skye could hear the sound of voices as she hurried up the path. She recognized Jake's deep tones and the higher ones of his sister, Wynne. She'd hoped to find him alone. She wasn't sure Wynne entirely approved of her.

Jake stood watching her approach. Skye thought that might be wariness in his expression, though what he had to be wary of in her, she didn't know.

"Looks like you've been working hard," Skye said, taking in the dirt on his face and the damp streak on the chest of his shirt.

"Yeah." His dark eyes watched her. "You feeling okay?"

"I wondered if I could talk to you a minute." What on earth was the matter with him? He almost acted like he was mad at her. They'd parted on good terms, especially after he'd saved her life.

"I guess I can spare a few minutes." He glanced toward Wynne, who seemed to be watching with great interest.

Wynne smiled. "Hi, Skye. Are you feeling okay?"

Skye's tension eased a bit at the other woman's friendly tone. "My head's still a little sore, but I'm okay." At least Wynne had seemed concerned, unlike her brother.

"Good. I've been praying for you."

Skye was taken back a bit at Wynne's comment. How kind of her. She could use all the prayers she could get. "Thanks."

Jake said nothing, and Skye frowned. Had he been praying for her? She'd assumed he was a Christian since he'd come to church with the family. She studied him with new eyes. Why had she never noticed that cynical twist to his mouth? She needed to find out more before she got any closer to him. She decided to spill her request and get out of their way.

"You want to talk in private? I need to run to town after some more water and I could do it now rather than at dinner," Wynne said.

"No, that's fine. I could use more minds on the puzzle," Skye said.

"Puzzle?"

Jake sounded interested now, but Skye was fast losing

any real desire to share her problem with him. She'd come this far though, and there was no graceful way to escape.

"I don't know if you've seen Wilson New Moon around—he's a mentally challenged man in his forties. He's generally dressed in jeans, a flannel shirt and suspenders?"

Wynne frowned. "I don't think I've seen him, but Becca has mentioned him."

Skye nodded. "Molly, Max's daughter, loves him and his balsam airplanes."

"What about him?"

The boredom in Jake's voice suddenly infuriated Skye. "Never mind," she said, not caring what he thought of her. She turned to go back to her truck. She'd talk to the sheriff about it.

Jake caught her arm. "Sorry, I'm a little distracted today."

Skye stood with her head down, not looking at him. "I need to get back to town."

"I said I'm sorry. What about this guy?"

"He's been a bear all morning," Wynne said. "Don't mind him. He's not mad at you. I'm the one who ticked him off."

"I'm not mad!"

Skye and Wynne looked at one another. Wynne rolled her eyes, and Skye giggled.

Jake snorted. "If you two are going to make fun of me, I'll get back to work."

He didn't sound mad anymore, so Skye sneaked a

peek at him. His firm lips quirked up on the ends, and he was regarding her with an amused expression in his eyes.

"So what about this Wilson?" he prompted.

His tone had changed, and the tension eased from her shoulders. The old Jake was back. "I ran into him in the forest today. I'd wondered why I hadn't seen him around in a while." She explained her relationship with him, then plunged into her fears. "I think he might know who attacked me the other day."

"Me, you mean," Jake corrected.

"I don't think you're the target, Jake. Wilson warned me about Asibikaashi."

"Asibikaashi. Who's that?"

"It's an old Ojibwa legend. The goddess Asibikaashi is a Spider Woman who brought the sunlight and is the authoress of the dreamcatchers. She's not something to fear, but Wilson is terrified."

Wynne shivered. "Sounds creepy."

"Of course, we know there's no such thing, but Wilson is convinced. He has to have seen or heard something." Skye rubbed her hands up her arms, suddenly cold in spite of the hot sun beating down.

"You think it could be that Tallulah woman?" Jake wanted to know.

"That was the first person who crossed my mind," Skye admitted.

Jake glanced at his watch. "I think it's about time she and I had a talk. I got plenty of work accomplished today anyway."

In spite of his words, Skye heard the regret in his voice. "Why don't you go ahead and work while it's light? We could go see her after supper."

"No, it's fine," Jake assured her. "I want to get to the bottom of this. If this woman is really dangerous, we need to know about it. The sheriff was going to talk to her, but he's not likely to spill what she had to say."

Wynne glanced at Skye. "Did you tell the sheriff about what Wilson said?"

Skye hesitated then shook her head, her cheeks burning. She knew what Jake's sister would think—that she'd come straight to Jake instead of the sheriff. She could only hope Jake didn't read her as easily as Wynne.

"I'm sure he's a friend, but that sheriff seems pretty useless," Jake said. "He didn't seem all that concerned about someone attacking us."

"We don't have much crime here, so we're all pretty used to handling our own problems. The Ojibwa are an independent lot. Besides, he's used to bullets whizzing around from hunters from the mainland. The hunters sometimes shoot at anything that moves. Rocks seem pretty tame by comparison."

"Jake is worth ten sheriffs," Wynne said with a touch of amusement in her voice.

"I know," Skye said. She and Wynne shared a look of understanding, and Skye suddenly realized Jake's sister was an ally. Her heart gave a leap of gladness.

Skye's best friend Sarah had moved to Ontonagon a year ago, and Skye had felt the void. She could use a friend.

Jake glanced at the exposed eggs. "I'm not sure about leaving them unprotected," he said.

"I'll stay and keep working," Wynne said. "You two go see what you can find. And bring back some bottles of water when you come."

"I don't like leaving you here by yourself." Jake frowned and hesitated. "Even the miners are off for the weekend."

"I'll be fine," Wynne said. "You're not the target. It appears Skye is."

"Cameron might be back for the other eggs. You might be in the line of fire."

"I could call my cousin to come stay, too," Skye said. "Michael is big enough no one is liable to mess with him."

"Call him," Jake said.

"I'll be fine! You won't be gone that long."

Skye pulled her cell phone out and dialed her cousin's number. He didn't answer so she left a message asking him to come out to the mine.

"He's never away from his messages for long," she said. "I imagine he'll be here in a bit. I could help with the dig until he gets here."

"No, you won't." Wynne looked determined. "Go ahead to town. Cameron won't try anything again. He knows we're on to him."

"Yeah, you're probably right." Jake took Skye's arm. "Let's go. Call us if anything suspicious happens."

Skye didn't like leaving the diminutive young woman alone, but she followed Jake's lead. She glanced back from the parking lot and saw Wynne wave. Skye said a little prayer for God to watch over her newfound friend.

Chapter Seven

Skye drove the truck expertly along the rutted dirt road. Jake admired the way she handled the old vehicle in the curves.

"Did your dad teach you to drive? You drive like a man," he said.

"Is that a compliment?" She sounded amused.

"Yeah, I guess it was meant to be." He grinned. "Sorry, that was chauvinistic, wasn't it?"

"A little, but I won't hold it against you."

Jake's grin broadened. He liked the way she didn't stay mad long. She certainly had the right to, after the way he'd acted when she first showed up. She had a way of disarming him, and he wished he hadn't acted like a jerk.

Skye slowed at a narrow lane. The truck barely squeezed through the opening flanked by raspberry bushes. The lane wound back nearly half a mile through some of the most unkempt foliage Jake had ever seen. The truck bottomed out in several holes, and Skye winced every time the undercarriage scraped the dirt.

"You sure she lives back here? I'm surprised she manages to keep a vehicle running."

"She doesn't. She rides a bicycle. I think she pushes it out to the road from her house."

"She lives alone?"

"She does now that her son is dead. Her husband used to be the fire chief. He died in a big hotel blaze ten years ago. She moved out here then. This property had been in her family for years, and the house was in shambles. I imagine it still is."

"She sounds pretty weird." And scary. Jake was beginning to think Skye might be right about this woman.

The truck rounded one last curve, and the house came into view. It was barely more than a shack. Jake guessed it had been built by a fur trapper. There couldn't be more than one room under the sagging, moss-covered roof. A couple of goats munched on shrubs in front of the building, and several chickens scrabbled in the dirt.

Skye stopped the truck in front of the house. "Looks like she's here."

"How can you tell?"

Skye pointed toward a tripod set up over an open fire. "She's cooking."

The aroma of some kind of soup wafted to his nose, and he nodded. "Any chance she'll take a potshot at us?"

"I hope not. Maybe we should stay in the truck and just honk the horn."

She was a smart lady. He nodded and reached over to press the horn. She winced as the horn blared. The goats bleated and bounded away as chickens squawked and fluttered wildly toward the woods.

"That should make her mad," Skye laughed.

Jake shrugged. "I'm not letting you out of this truck until she shows her face."

Before Skye replied, Jake saw movement from the corner of his eye. He whipped his head around and saw what he would have called a mountain woman approach the truck. She wore worn dungarees, boots and a faded shirt that might have been red once. A floppy hat even more decrepit than the one on Jake's head perched atop gray braids.

"Stop that!" Tallulah said. She slapped the hood of the truck with a dirty hand. "You're scaring my livestock." She glowered at them and jerked open Skye's door. "If you want to talk to me, then get out of there."

Skye glanced at Jake, and he shrugged. "She doesn't seem to be armed," he whispered.

Skye nodded and got out. Jake followed suit. He watched Tallulah warily, ready to jump her if she pulled a weapon.

"Sorry to bother you, Tallulah," Skye said. "We wondered if you'd seen Wilson lately."

"No, I haven't. If you see him, tell him to come and get those airplanes out of my house." She glowered at Skye. "You have the nerve to show up here after killing my boy."

"I'm sorry about Robert," Skye said.

Jake thought he saw tears in Skye's eyes. On the drive out, she'd talked about how close she was to Robert. Too bad Tallulah didn't seem to realize Skye was genuinely cut up about the teen's death.

"A lot of good your sorry does." She clenched and unclenched her fists.

"You have some of Wilson's planes here?" Skye's voice was nonchalant, but she glanced at Jake with a gleam in her eye.

"Robert liked to work with him on them. The last ones they built are still by my fireplace. I want them gone." Tallulah's voice softened. "Though I might keep one."

Skye was being too gentle, Jake decided. "You been out to the garnet mine lately?"

She didn't answer, just stared at them. "I want you off my property. You done sicced the law on me."

So the sheriff had at least come out and talked to her. That was progress. Jake didn't like the angry glint in her eyes. She might be as dangerous as Skye suspected. "We're trying to figure out who tried to hurt Skye."

"You got no call to talk to me like I'm some kind of criminal. I haven't hurt anyone."

"I heard you tried to shake Skye from a ladder a few weeks ago, attacked her, too. She said you threatened to kill her."

"She's a murderer," Tallulah snapped. "With your mouth, maybe someone was trying to hurt you and not her. You seem the type to make enemies."

He grinned wryly. "And you seem a good judge of character, ma'am."

She regarded him soberly as if she thought he was making fun of her, but her wary expression didn't fade.

"We don't want to keep you from your work," Skye

said. "Did we disturb you?"

Her placating tone seemed to work a bit. Tallulah looked eager. "You want to see my babies?"

Jake assumed she meant baby chickens or goats. "Sure." Feeling magnanimous, he touched Skye's waist and guided her ahead of him. They followed Tallulah to a shed behind the house. The door had a shiny padlock on it, and Tallulah fished out a key from the pocket of her jeans.

She unlocked it and pushed open the door. "Go ahead," she said.

Jake felt Skye stiffen and stop in the doorway. She uttered a small sound, like a strangled scream. He glanced over her shoulder.

A counter held glass cages in rows. Snakes coiled one on top of each other. The nearest cage held a huge snake that rattled and struck at them from the other side of the glass.

Skye gasped and rushed past Jake. He followed her and found her with her hands over her eyes. She was shaking.

"I hate snakes," she said, turning and burying her face against his chest.

He held her until her trembling began to subside.

Tallulah laughed. "You don't like my babies? How interesting." Her eyes had a derisive gleam as if she'd known all along how Skye would react.

"What are you doing with all those snakes?" Jake demanded. He softened his tone. "You must have a hundred timber rattlers in there."

"Aren't you afraid of getting bit?" Skye asked.

"I know how to handle them," the other woman said. "But they can be dangerous. They like to bite." Her dark gaze stayed on Skye's face.

"Could Robert have been bitten?" Jake asked.

An expression of horror crossed Tallulah's face. "He knew better than to mess with them snakes. Besides, he would have told me."

"Maybe he was afraid because he knew he wasn't supposed to handle them." Jake knew he wouldn't have told his mom. Kids that age thought they were invincable. Robert might have thought he'd just be sick a while, then get over it.

Tallulah was shaking her head. "Don't you go trying to confuse me," she muttered. "It was Skye. She gave me bad herbs." She took her hat off and rubbed her forehead. "Just get out of here," she growled. "And don't come back." Her back stiff, she turned around and went back into the snake shack. She pulled the door shut behind her with a slam.

"I guess we've been dismissed," Jake said. "Still sure it wasn't her?"

"She still seems a little—deranged."

"She gives me the willies."

Skye nodded. "I guess we should talk to the sheriff again."

"We could tell him what Wilson said, but he probably can't do anything. There's no proof it's Tallulah."

"Let's get come coffee. My head hurts from thinking about it."

They drove toward town. Rounding a curve, she saw a flash of movement.

"It's Wilson!" Skye pulled the truck to a stop and jumped out. "Wilson, I want to talk to you."

The big man froze where he was picking berries. "I wasn't doing nothing, Skye."

"I know."

Jake followed her as she approached the man. He was filthy and his clothes hung on him as though he'd lost a lot of weight.

"I went to see Tallulah," Skye said. "Have you seen her lately?"

"She has some of my planes," Wilson said.

"Is she the Spider Woman?" Skye asked.

Wilson pointed a finger at Skye. "You stay away." He turned and plunged into the forest.

They shouted after him but he didn't stop. "That didn't accomplish much," Jake said. "Let's go get some coffee." They drove to town, and then sipped their java and talked. He found himself too engrossed in watching Skye's face as she talked about her childhood.

His cell phone rang and he answered it. He glanced at his watch and was surprised to see they'd been at the coffee shop over an hour and a half. "Baxter."

"Jake, you'd better get to the hospital." Becca's voice sounded strained. "Someone attacked Wynne out at the site."

Skye drove at breakneck speed to town. She'd had a funny feeling about leaving Wynne at the site by herself. She should have listened to her intuition. This was all her fault. When would she learn not to involve other people in her problems?

"I'm sorry, Jake," she said. "I shouldn't have dragged you away from the site."

"Don't blame yourself," he said. "I knew better than to leave her alone. I shouldn't have left until some help got there. Your cousin found her. If we'd just waited a little while, this wouldn't have happened. I was all set on playing the hero and didn't use good sense."

He sounded grim. Skye bit her lip. "Did Becca say how badly Wynne was hurt?"

"A broken leg for sure. She's still with the doctor."

Skye winced. "She won't be much help on the dig. Would you let me take her place? You're going to need someone."

"I'm not sure I want you anywhere around," he said. "You might be bad luck. Everywhere you go, trouble seems to follow."

Skye didn't blame him, but his words still stung. Her eyes burned, and she stared straight ahead.

"Hey, I was just joking." Jake touched her arm. "You can help if you have time. I'd be glad for the company at least."

He obviously didn't think her much help and was trying to placate her. She didn't reply. Maybe his joke was closer to the truth than he knew. Could God be trying to tell her not to pursue any friendship with Jake? Sparks seemed to fly whenever the two of them met and someone got hurt. That couldn't be good.

"It could have been Tallulah," she said. "Maybe we made her mad today. We were gone for over an hour and a half. That's plenty of time for her to have attacked Wynne."

Jake shook his head. "I'm more inclined to believe it's Cameron."

She pulled into the hospital parking lot and parked in the outpatient section. Jake was out of the truck almost before she had it stopped. He took off at a dead run toward the emergency room entrance.

Skye ran after him. She'd been praying for Wynne the whole time she'd been driving. If Wynne was seriously injured, Skye would never forgive herself.

The Baxter family was gathered in the waiting room. Becca stood in the circle of her husband Max's arms. Gram sat on a love seat, and Jake's cousin Tate paced the floor. Skye didn't see Molly, Max's young daughter.

"Jake!" Becca flew into her brother's embrace.

He soothed her and led her to a sofa beside their grandmother. "What happened?"

Becca was still sobbing softly, so Max answered. "She was working when someone jumped her from above. Her leg broke from the guy's weight."

"Did she get a look at him?"

Max shrugged, his anxious gaze on his wife. "The guy had a nylon stocking over his face. She said it happened too fast to get more than an impression that it was a man. Once her leg broke, she passed out from the pain."

"Any other injuries?" Skye put in. When everyone's

gaze turned to her, she wished she'd kept her mouth shut. Maybe they all blamed her.

"Cuts and bruises. But the break is a bad one. They've taken her to surgery," Gram said. She leaned over from her place on the love seat. "Sit here by me, Skye dear. You look distraught."

Skye allowed the older woman to pull her down onto the love seat. "I like Wynne," she said. "I shouldn't have involved Jake in my problems."

"Nonsense," Gram said. "Jake is a good one to turn to in times of trouble. I'm sure he was only too happy to rescue a damsel in distress."

Jake was paying no attention to them. Skye watched him pace the waiting room and knew he couldn't wait to see his sister with his own eyes and question her about what happened. Skye pitied the man who had attacked Wynne. Once Jake discovered the attacker's identity, the man would wish he'd never been born.

The sheriff entered the waiting room. "I hear there's been another attack out at the mine," he said. He took his notebook out of his pocket. "Anyone want to tell me what happened?"

Max explained the circumstances. Jake glanced at Skye with a question in his eyes, and she nodded her head. The sheriff might as well be informed of everything, though she didn't think Wynne's attack was related to Wilson's warning.

Jake plunged into the story as soon as Max finished.

"I'll see if I can find Wilson," the sheriff said, putting away his pen and paper.

101

Molly, Max's daughter, came from the direction of the bathroom. Her face brightened when she saw Skye and she ran to her.

"Did you bring anything with you for making dream-catchers?" she asked hopefully. "I've been practicing since you showed me how."

Skye smiled. "I might have some thread in the truck," she said. It might help them all pass the time. "I'll get it." She went to the truck and got her basket of materials from behind the truck seat.

By the time she got back inside, Jake had disap-peared.

Becca saw her quick glance. "Jake went back to see Wynne. They wheeled her by on the way to surgery, and you know Jake. He insisted on accompanying her so he could talk to her. Wynne looked too out of it to be much help in explaining anything." Her frown was troubled. "The doctor says she'll be fine though."

A flood of relief washed over Skye. "Thank God."

"Amen," Becca said. She smiled at Skye. "Are you going to teach us all how to make a dreamcatcher?"

"Sure, if you want to learn." She set her small basket on the coffee table in front of an empty sofa. Molly crowded beside her on the sofa while Becca got on the other side.

Skye explained the knots. "Tell us about dream-catchers," Molly demanded.

"You've already heard the story." Skye smiled at the child's eagerness.

"Tell me again. Becca doesn't know about them. I

tried to tell her but I forgot part of it."

Skye smiled. "The Spider Women, Asibikaashi, built dreamcatchers over the heads of children to catch the good dreams in the night. When the Ojibwa Nation dispersed to the four corners of North America, to fill a prophecy, Asibikaashi had a difficult time making her journey to all those cradle boards, so the mothers, sisters and grandmothers took up the practice of weaving the magical webs for the new babies. We traditionally use willow hoops and sinew made from plants."

"Why is it in a circle?" Molly wanted to know.

"The circle represents how *giizis,* the sun, travels each day across the sky. The dreamcatcher will filter out all the bad *bawedjigewin,* or dreams, and allow only good thoughts to enter into our minds."

"And all the circles?" Becca asked.

"As the dreams travel through the web, good dreams are permitted to pass through and flow to the feather's tip, to the owner of the web. Bad dreams become so lost among the maze that when the morning sun comes up, still lost in the web, they are destroyed by the strongest of the early morning light."

Molly was practically bouncing with excitement. "I want one for over my bed."

"And you shall have one. This one will be yours," Skye promised. "But you know it is only a legend. Jesus keeps us safe. Bad dreams can't harm us."

"I know." Molly nodded.

Jake came back looking disgruntled as Skye finished the legend. "She doesn't remember anything else."

"I tried to tell you." Becca stood and went to the coffee station. She handed her brother a cup. "Sit down. It's going to be at least a couple of hours, the doctor said."

He accepted the cup. His gaze collided with Skye's, and she wished she could ease the frustrated fear she saw in his face. She smiled, and his face cleared. He joined her on the sofa. "That's a pretty pattern," he said.

Skye had been continuing her dreamcatcher knots without even noticing she was working. "Thanks."

The sheriff's cell phone rang. He answered it and listened for a few moments then clicked it off. He looked at Skye. "You'd better get home, Skye. Your mamma called and someone broke into your shop. There's been quite a bit of destruction."

Chapter Eight

The front door of The Sleeping Turtle hung ajar. Bits of shattered glass crunched beneath Skye's sneakers as she entered the shop. She felt as though someone had rifled through her journal or her private desk, and the violation made her feel physically sick. Jake's fingers pressing reassuringly against her arm was the only thing that kept her moving forward through the vandalism.

For wanton vandalism was what it surely was. There was a viciousness in the way her dreamcatchers had been ripped apart. Bundles of herbs looked as though they had been stomped on with deliberate and destructive glee. Glass lay smashed and papers from their files were tossed around like confetti.

"Who would do this?" Skye whispered. "Does someone hate me that much?"

"I know it looks bad, Skye," Sheriff Mitchell said. "But it was likely just kids having a spree."

"You can say that after the way she was attacked?" Jake's voice rose, and he shot the sheriff a look of incredulity.

The sheriff raised his eyebrows. "I doubt it's related. We've seen this sort of thing before. School is almost out for the summer, and we often see kids vandalizing store windows and cars."

"This goes beyond mere vandalism."

Skye could hear the anger rising in Jake's voice. She managed a smile and pressed his hand. "It's okay, maybe he's right, Jake. Everything isn't necessarily connected."

The skeptical look he gave her proclaimed his opinion on the matter, but he didn't say anything. "Can I clean it up?" she asked the sheriff.

"Let me check it out first. You can clean it up tomorrow."

Meaning he didn't intend to look very hard. Skye suppressed a sigh. Maybe she and Jake could find some clues in the mess. Glancing at her watch, she nodded briskly. Jake needed to be back at the hospital when Wynne came out of surgery. Besides, if she stayed here, she was likely to throttle the sheriff and land in jail herself.

Her mother came rushing in the door. Peter followed her. Skye turned with a glad cry. "Mother!" She felt like a little girl who wanted her mommy to kiss the boo-boos and make it all better.

Her mother rushed to Skye and hugged her. "Oh, Skye, I'm so sorry. Look at this mess." She sounded near tears.

"I know." Skye tried to swallow the lump in her throat, but it kept bounding back. "All our work. This will take months to replace."

"Oh honey, I wish I could fix it," Peter said. He put a meaty arm around each woman.

Skye felt her burden ease with her stepfather's appearance. He would move heaven and earth to get them the supplies necessary to replace what had been destroyed. She could always count on him, unlike her real father. A fierce longing for her father swept over her at the thought, which made no sense. Peter had always been here for her.

She returned his hug with more enthusiasm than usual. He did so much, and she hardly ever thanked him for it.

"We'll see about getting you a loan to get back on your feet," he said. "Minimal interest, too."

"Thanks, Peter, but I don't think I'll need it. Surely insurance will cover it."

"That's true," he conceded. "I just want to do something to help."

"Just being here for me helps in ways you can't imagine," she said.

He patted her shoulder. "I'm glad." He turned and saw Jake wandering through the rubble. "What's he doing here?" he whispered. "Have you been seeing him?"

"He was with me when I heard the news and came along to see if he could help out. We both seem to be targets lately."

"I doubt it's related, though, unless someone is trying to warn you to stay away from him."

"It looks more like it might be the other way around. Someone attacked me in the mine. The rocks were probably from the same person."

Her mother chewed on her lip. "I'm worried, Skye. Maybe you should go stay with your aunt Margaret on the mainland for a while. It will take weeks for the insurance to release the money to repair the damage here. You could spend the time looking through stores to replace stock, go on a buying trip to New York, maybe."

What her mother said made sense, but Skye shook her head. "I'm not running away. I want to find out who's doing this and why. None of it makes sense." A thought occurred to her and she glanced up at Peter. "You said you would be willing to give me a loan. Maybe I'll take you up on that."

She couldn't tell him what she would use it for just yet. A smile played at the corners of her lips.

"You look like you're up to something," her mother said.

"I'm just excited about the future. Maybe this is a blessing in disguise," Skye said, gaining control of her features.

She wanted to rush her mother and Peter out of the shop and call James. He would be thrilled at her idea.

He would be the only one in approval.

She brushed away the thought like a worrisome black fly. She knew it would work, too. James and Michael would make sure it worked. They were driven to turn the mine around. They'd throw everything they had into the plan.

"There's not much we can do here now," Skye said. "I'd better take Jake back to the hospital."

Jake was near enough to overhear. He glanced at his watch in agreement. "Wynne should be out of surgery within another half an hour or so. I'd probably better get back." He nodded to Skye's mother and stepfather. "I'm sorry about this."

"Thanks for being such a good friend to our Skye," her mother said. "You'll have to come to dinner one night. We like to get to know her friends."

Surprise rippled across his face, and he flushed. "We've been trying to help one another out. I'm afraid I'll be too busy with the dig to make any social engagements."

Skye thought the comment was meant to make it clear they were allies only, not friends, and certainly nothing more. She wanted to crawl under the counter. What must Jake think? He surely assumed her mother's comment meant Skye had told her mother things about

108

their relationship that weren't true. No wonder Jake looked embarrassed.

"Let's go, Jake," she said with as much brusqueness as she could manage. She would have to show him their relationship was strictly as associates with no personal stakes involved.

Jake nodded distantly and went to the door. His face was a stiff mask, and his jaw was tight. Skye wanted to cry or scream, she wasn't sure which. She hugged her mother and Peter and followed Jake out the door.

The silence as they drove back to the hospital was unnerving. Skye couldn't stand more than five minutes of it. "Look, I know how my mother's comment sounded, but believe me, I've given her no reason to think we have a relationship."

Jake didn't reply for a few long moments. Skye held her breath, wondering if she'd gone too far by bringing things into the open.

"I'm sorry I was curt with her," he said. "And you're a nice girl, Skye, but I move around too much to even think of getting into a relationship. I tried it once and that was enough."

"What happened?" The words were out before she could snatch them back.

"I'd rather not talk about it."

She'd been nicely slapped back into place. Skye bit her lip. "Okay. Sorry."

He gave a heavy sigh. "No, I'm sorry. It's not something I like to remember. I dated a research student for a summer. I thought she would want to join the team on a permanent basis and travel the world with me. She informed me she wanted me to join the professor pool at the university in her hometown. She had the house all picked out near the campus."

"I'm sorry." Now more than ever, Skye could see there would never be a future for her with this man. She couldn't imagine leaving Eagle Island. It was as much a part of her as the color of her hair and the gray flecks in her dark eyes. Leaving here would be like ripping out a part of who she was.

"I was, too, for a while." He grimaced. "It was for the best. I'm the rambling kind of guy. Maybe I always will be."

At least he was warning her of the truth. That fact proved to her he felt some kind of attraction for her. It was a small crumb of comfort. "I could never leave here," she admitted. "So it's just as well we had this little talk."

She felt a small thrill of satisfaction when she saw the disappointment on his face. He'd evidently told her to see her reaction. Had he hoped she'd say she had always wanted to see the world? Some women would, she knew. Most of the women on the island complained about the small world the island offered and dreamed of far-flung, exotic locales.

She stopped the truck in front of the hospital. "I hope Wynne is okay."

"You're not coming in?"

She shook her head. "I need to run out to the mine before the second shift men leave. There's something I need to discuss with Pop."

"Why am I afraid?" He grinned. "You've got an expression that says something is brewing in that smart head of yours."

"Maybe." She found herself smiling back at him. Their little talk had cleared the air between them. Maybe they would now be free to be real friends. Though the thought should have made her happy, she found a trace of depression creeping in. She'd hoped for more, though she hadn't admitted it to herself.

"What are you up to?"

"I'm not telling yet. I need to see if it's a possibility. This day could turn out to be a blessing in disguise."

He shook his head. "You're nuts."

"Maybe. We'll see." Giving a little salute with her fingers, she drove off and left him standing on the sidewalk. She looked in the rearview mirror and saw him wave as he headed toward the door.

She called James's house and his wife told Skye he was at the mine. She drove the ten miles out to the mine and parked beside James's car, then went inside.

James's feet sat atop a stack of papers on his desk, and he leaned back in his chair with his hands behind his head. He saw her and sat up so sharply, he knocked the stack of papers over. "What are you doing here?"

"I might ask you the same thing, Pop. You work too hard. Though you don't look too busy at the moment." Quickly she explained what had happened to her shop.

"Why are you looking so excited? I would have expected you to be upset." He eyed her suspiciously.

"I was, at first. Then Peter offered me a loan." She gave him a slow smile and winked.

His jaw slackened, and his mouth fell open. "Are you thinking what I think you're thinking?"

"Yep. The insurance money will cover replacing the store stock. Peter didn't say what I had to use the loan money for."

"The Mitchell tube," they said in unison.

James leaped from his chair and tossed her a high-five. "You're brilliant! You realize he's going to be mad when he finds out you are opening the Mitchell tube?"

"I know, Pop." She sobered. "That's the only thing about the plan I hate. Peter has been so good to me and Mother. He's just so stubborn on this subject. I know the tube badly needs to be shored up, but I think we can make it safer. And it won't take long to find out if we're right and the diamonds are there. If they are, we'll have no trouble convincing an investor to give us enough money to explore it properly."

"I like the way your mind works." James's face was flushed and his smile lit the room. "When can we get the money?"

"Peter talked like he could run it through right away because the insurance would take so long."

"What about the store?"

"I'm okay to let it ride until the insurance money comes through. The things that will take the longest to replace are the dreamcatchers, and I have to make them myself, so they'll take months anyway. This will work."

"I know it will." He grabbed her hands, and they did a jig around the office floor. "I was beginning to think you were losing heart, Skye."

"I was. But not any longer. We're going to do this, Pop."

"I need to order the supplies." He suddenly looked worried. "I hope Peter doesn't blame me."

"I'll make sure he knows it was all my doing," she promised.

"What about your mother? The mine belongs to her."

"And she trusts me with the running of it."

"What if she puts her foot down when she sees what we're doing and tells you to shut it down?"

"I think I can talk her out of it. She doesn't totally let Peter rule the roost at home. Remember how she let the paleontologists start digging over his objections? If she knows how much it means to me, she'll agree to let me try. It's not like we're doing a full extraction."

"No, this is just enough to see if a full one is feasible," he agreed. "But we both believe in it, Skye."

"I know those diamonds are there," she said. "Now we just have to find them."

Chapter Nine

Wynne's usual high spirits over the next few days brought Jake relief. He skipped church to be with her, but not even a broken leg was able to keep her down for long, and he was able to concentrate on his dig during the first part of the week and prepare to meet Kimball Washington.

Wednesday brought clear, sunny skies, and Jake waited at the dock for the ferry. Kimball was standing at the railing. Dressed in a tweed suit and cap, he looked every bit the college professor. His chocolate-colored skin glowed with health, and his dark eyes brightened at the sight of Jake waving to him.

He stepped off the ferry and grasped Jake's hand then pulled him into a brief hug. "Jake, you're a sight for sore eyes." He fell into step beside Jake and tugged his rolling suitcase along. "I'm eager to see this site of yours."

"I can't wait to show you." He introduced Kimball to Max, who shook the professor's hand, then took the luggage from him.

"I'm sure you two have plenty of work to do. I told Jake I'd take your luggage on home so you can get out to the site."

"Excellent. Give me a minute to change my clothes." Kimball's voice was eager.

"Lovely island," Kimball remarked as Jake drove along the rocky coastline out to the dig.

"Yes, it is." Jake parked the SUV. "I'm glad you're here, Kimball. I need all the help I can get." As they walked up the path to the dig, he told him what had been going on and the eggs he'd found.

"Paleontology can be a cutthroat business," Kimball said. "The sooner it's announced, the better. We can get a team together to fully excavate the site, set up security and manage what goes on."

"That's what I thought." Jake stepped to his eggs and pointed. "There they are."

Kimball rubbed his hands together. "Let's hatch one of these babies. That will rocket the discovery to the front page of the newspapers." He set down his satchel and pulled out two tiny microscopes as well as several small chisels. "If we can confirm what dinosaur we're dealing with, this could get exciting. These are the largest eggs I've seen."

The eggs were nearly twenty inches long, and Jake had been eager to learn what he had here. He knelt beside Kimball, and they began to work on freeing the largest egg from the cluster where it had been found.

Within an hour, the egg was loose. "Help me lift it. We'll put it on that rock ledge so we don't have to stoop to work on it." Kimball nodded his head toward a nearby flat ledge.

Grunting, Jake helped him carry the heavy egg to the rock. It was the perfect height for further work. "How long do think it will take?" He knew the chipping away of rock to "hatch" what was inside was painstaking work.

"At least a month," Kimball said.

Jake winced. "We have to protect this for a month? Maybe we should move to Windigo Manor, where it's more able to be watched."

"Might be a good idea," Kimball agreed. "But let's work a little longer today and see what we can chip loose."

Several times as they worked over the egg, Jake felt the back of his neck prickle as though he was being watched. He looked around occasionally but saw nothing, but his unease continued as the sun cast long shadows over the site.

Around six he looked at his watch. "Let's quit for supper. We can take the egg with us to town."

"What about the others?"

"It's getting dark enough that I don't think anyone can chisel them loose."

"I don't think you realize what you've got here," Kimball said.

"What are you thinking?" Jake hoped his friend would concur with his own speculations.

"As big as the eggs are, I suspect it might be a Sauroposeidon or something even larger. The wonders we might find at this site boggle my mind."

The eagerness in his friend's voice told Jake this find might be truly monumental. His own excitement kicked up a notch. "I'd hoped you'd say that and wasn't my own wishful thinking. When can we announce this?"

"Not until I can identify the bones in this egg. We

have to be very careful not to let any leaks out until the right time."

Jake scowled. "It's possible Reynolds might excavate the eggs he stole and announce it first."

Kimball winced. "Then we're going to have to work faster. I'm willing to work twenty hours a day if necessary."

"Me, too." Jake set his jaw. There was no way he was going to let Cameron Reynolds steal this discovery, too.

Skye sat across the desk from Peter. The shiny, expansive surface made her feel detached from her stepfather. She hadn't often come to his office, and the distance felt disconcerting.

Peter pushed the papers across the desk to her. "Sign here."

She scrawled her signature and tried to ignore the guilt knocking against her ribs. She should have been upfront with her stepfather about what she intended to use the money for, but he hadn't asked. If he had questioned her, she would have told him the truth.

Excitement crawled along her spine as he handed her the check with a smile. "Glad I could help."

"You're a peach, Peter," she said, rising from the slick, leather chair.

"Your mother wants you to stop by on your way home. She found some new items she thought you might want to order for the shop."

"Okay." She thought about telling him what she was going to do with the money, but decided maybe she'd better deposit the funds first. Then he couldn't do anything to stop her. But guilt wouldn't be kept quiet for long. She'd have to confess.

She exited Peter's office, stopped off at the counter, deposited the check, then hurried to her truck. James would be thrilled. He had an order ready to go for equipment to start the extraction of the Mitchell tube.

But first she'd better get her mother on board. She drove to her mother's and went inside. "Hello!" she called in the hallway.

"In here, Skye." Her mother's voice echoed from the kitchen.

Skye sniffed and the aroma of beef pasties wafted to her nose. Her stomach rumbled at the mixed scent of beef, pie crust, potato and rutabaga. "I hope those are about ready. I'm starved," she said, walking into the kitchen. She stopped when she saw her cousin Michael seated at the table, too.

"Hey, Skye." He swiped the gravy from his chin.

"Help yourself." Her mother pushed one toward her. "They're fresh from the oven."

Skye slid one to a plate and cut into it with a fork. The beef juice spilled out and she took a bite. "Um, delicious." She hadn't eaten breakfast.

"You get everything taken care of with Peter?" her mother asked.

"Yep." Skye took another bite.

"Good. I have some things I want to order for the shop."

"You might wait on that just yet. I have some other

plans for the money."

"Oh?"

"James and I have been talking about that Mitchell tube. We're both convinced if there are diamonds at the mine, they are down that tube." She sent Michael a warning glance.

"Peter says it's dangerous. And what does that have to do with the money you got from the bank?"

Michael cleared his throat. "We really think we can extract a small sample without any danger. If we can find a few diamonds, we can get some investors and shore up the tube to fully extract it."

Skye nodded. "And I want to use this money to run a sample extraction."

Her mother's eyes widened. "Did you tell Peter?"

"No, I wanted to talk to you about it first. It's your mine." Skye leaned forward. "I have to do this, Mother. Until we check out that tube, I can't let go of it. Daddy would have pressed forward and found out for sure. We have to have the courage to do the same."

"Your father is gone, Skye. It's time you realized that."

"I know. But if we find diamonds, it would be tremendously beneficial for our tribe. We could hire a lot of other Ojibwa to work it and really make a difference here."

"That's true." Her mother looked thoughtful. "Peter won't like it."

Michael jumped in again. "I promise it won't be dangerous. James will make sure of that."

"I don't know." Her mother seemed unconvinced. "Maybe it's time we closed the mine. I know Peter would like to see it continue, but maybe it's time."

"You'd be firing a lot of good men if you did that," Michael pointed out. "And there aren't many places for them to find other jobs. Let's not give up yet."

Her mother looked suddenly decisive. "Okay, we'll try it." She glanced from Michael to Skye. "But you have to promise that if you find nothing after the money is gone, you'll give it up. There's no sense in beating a dead horse."

"I promise." Skye felt it safe to make that promise. She had a feeling in her bones that things were about to change at the mine.

"You got it." Michael got up from the table. "I have to run. Thanks for the pasty, Aunt Mary." He kissed her on the cheek and waved at Skye, then went out the back door.

Her mother turned back to Skye. "Becca ordered a welcome basket for a guest. Would you mind taking it to Windigo Manor?"

The innocence on her mother's face didn't fool Skye. "Mother, you're matchmaking again. There can never be anything between me and Jake Baxter."

Her mother made no pretense of denying the accusation. "He's a fine man, Skye. I don't understand your attitude."

"I don't want to leave Eagle Island, and Jake isn't the type to settle down in one place. Besides, I'm not sure about his beliefs."

"He has come to church with the rest of the family."

"And that's all. Church attendance doesn't mean he's a believer."

"You need to find out," her mother declared. "And there's no better time than the present. Besides, much as I'd miss you, you need to get out and see the world."

"I love my home here." Skye heard the defensiveness in her voice.

"But your attachment isn't healthy. It's almost as if you're afraid to leave. You think one day your father is going to walk back through that door, and you want to be here when he does. That's right, isn't it?" Her mother's voice was gentle.

A bulge formed in Skye's throat. "Maybe. Is that so wrong? He's out there somewhere, Mother. Someday maybe he'll miss us enough to come back."

Her mother sighed. "Oh, Skye, it's never going to happen. Your father has a new life somewhere. He's forgotten all about us. I'm sorry if that sounds harsh, but you have to face facts. He walked away and never looked back."

"But *why?* I've never understood that."

"Neither have I. But things were rocky between him and me. It wasn't your fault, but mine."

"Then why did he never call me? No birthday card, nothing." Skye blinked rapidly. She would not humiliate herself by crying now.

Her mother shrugged. "Your father always walked a different path. He was a dreamer. There was always another pot of gold waiting for him under a new rainbow."

"He seemed happy enough here. And he was excited about the mine. He really believed he'd find diamonds there someday."

"Maybe he finally woke up about that mine. You have to do the same."

Skye rose. "Not until I explore the Mitchell tube."

"Fine. If that's what it takes to make you face reality, you have my blessing." Her mother handed her the basket filled with Ojibwa handicrafts. "Don't forget to drop this off at Windigo Manor on your way."

Skye took the basket and hurried to her truck. No matter what her mother said, she wasn't giving up just yet.

She hadn't seen Jake since the day her shop was broken into, and she felt jittery as she drove the truck to the Manor. Silly really. Jake would likely be at the dig. She turned into the driveway and caught her breath. Jake's SUV sat in front of the house. She glanced at her watch. Wonder what he was doing home in the middle of the afternoon? His friend and mentor had arrived a few days ago, and she'd assumed they'd spend every waking hour at work.

She almost turned tail to run. It would be so easy to whip the truck around and hightail it out of there before anyone saw her, but her mother would know if she didn't get the basket delivered. Maybe she could just drop it off with the housekeeper and get out before anyone noticed her.

She parked behind Jake's vehicle and grabbed the basket. Her chest felt tight and hard as she went up the brick walk to the front door. The imposing mansion seemed to jeer at her. She could never be part of a family like this even if Jake was willing to settle down here. Her roots went to Ojibwa hogans and long treks in the forest.

Her heart thumping against her ribs, she pressed the doorbell and waited. Becca opened the door, and her welcoming smile was like balm on Skye's soul.

"Skye, I was just talking about you. Come in." Becca didn't wait for a response but took Skye's arm and pulled her inside. "Hey, everyone, look who's here." She tugged on Skye's arm and led her to the living room.

Skye followed reluctantly. She should have insisted her mother bring the stupid basket.

Her gaze connected with Jake's as she entered the room. He stood beside a handsome African-American man whose eyes widened appreciatively when he saw Skye. Was that a welcoming smile on Jake's face or a grimace? She couldn't tell.

Standing uneasily in the doorway, she shifted her basket to the other hand. "Mother asked me to drop this basket off," she said.

"Oh, that's for Kimball." Becca took the basket from Skye. "Kimball, this is Skye Blackbird. She's Ojibwa royalty and can tell you all about the native culture on the island. She owns The Sleeping Turtle and makes wonderful dreamcatchers." She turned to Skye. "Kimball is a professor at the University of Chicago. He's helping Jake with the dig."

"Hello." Skye still wanted to run. She hardly dared look at Jake. The last exchange between them was still too painful. He'd made his lack of interest in her quite clear.

"I've been wanting to show you what we've found, Skye." Jake came toward her and took her arm. "It's in the basement."

Her arm tingled where he touched her, and she pulled away from him. She tempered her reaction with a smile. "Lead the way."

His face changed as though she'd slapped him, but he didn't say anything. He went past her to the hall and led her through the kitchen to the basement entrance. Flicking on the light switch, he went down the steps, and she followed.

"Look at the size of that egg." He pointed to a large, oval-shaped stone on the workbench. It had been chiseled away, and tiny bone fragments lay exposed.

Skye approached the egg. "What is it, do you know?"

"Kimball thinks it might be the largest egg discovered to date. If we could find adult bones in the same area, we might be able to identify an entirely new dinosaur."

"Congratulations." The words practically choked her. "When will you be announcing this?"

"Probably not for at least two more weeks. We'd thought it might take a month, but we've been working practically round the clock and it's going quickly."

Jake stood closer than was comfortable for Skye's

state of mind. "I'm about to start work in a new tube at the mine. You're going to close us down, aren't you?"

The elation faded on Jake's face. "That might happen, yes. I'm sorry."

"I'll fight you. You know that." She turned and stared into his face.

"I know." He stood looking down at her, and the expression on his face changed.

She saw the way his nostrils flared and his eyes darkened. Then he bent his head and kissed her.

She couldn't deny she'd wondered what it would be like to kiss Jake Baxter, but she wasn't prepared for the tide of emotion that swept over her like a tsunami. She wrapped her fingers in his chambray shirt and held on for dear life. This man evoked emotions in her she'd never felt. He wasn't safe, though he made her feel protected.

The scent of his cologne made her feel dizzy, and the touch of his lips penetrated the defenses she'd thought invulnerable. Even through the onslaught of emotions, she knew she should pull away and run up the steps behind her, but she couldn't move. She'd never been faced with this kind of temptation before and knew she was failing miserably.

With a supreme effort, she tore her mouth free and stepped back. She touched her fingertips to her lips. They felt warm from Jake's kiss. "Why did you do that?"

"I don't know." He ran his hand through his hair.

"Don't do it again." She tried to make her voice stern

then turned and dashed up the steps, tripping over the top one. She raced past Kimball Washington with a murmur of apology and made it to the safety of her truck. She'd just made a complete fool of herself.

Chapter Ten

Jake had hired a guard, a surly, stout Ojibwa named Joe, whom Skye swore would defend the site with his life. Joe didn't say much, but Jake never caught him sleeping or goofing off when he was supposed to be watching. With his leather vest and hat decorated with a single feather, Joe reminded Jake of the native scouts who used to lead the settlers West.

Jake couldn't deny he kept watch for Skye. The dig looked down on the entrance to the mine, and he found his gaze straying in that direction every few minutes. A thousand times he had castigated himself for scaring her off that way. She'd made it clear how she felt by the way she tore out of the basement a week ago. If he'd entertained a slim hope that there could be anything between them, the thought had died as he watched her retreat up the stairs.

He pushed away the thoughts plaguing his mind and went up the slope to the dig. "Morning, Joe. Any trouble last night?"

The stocky native shook his head. "Nothing, Jake. Pretty quiet night."

"Go get some rest. I'm going to work on releasing a

few more eggs today. Don't come running if you hear another vehicle midmorning. Kimball's due in then."

Joe nodded and went to the tent in a grassy knoll in the meadow. The June sun was hot, so Jake took off his chambray shirt and pulled on a T-shirt. Adrenaline pumped through his blood as he knelt by the clutch of eggs again.

They seemed to get larger as he went deeper into the ground. What else was hidden on this slope? In his mind's eye, he could see the entire hillside excavated. Maybe the largest dinosaur bones found to date would be uncovered here. This spot was what he'd been searching for all his life—the fame he sought slept here, just under the surface of the soil.

His chest expanded as he contemplated the future. Lecture invitations, elite digs, magazine and newspaper articles, maybe the front page of *Time* and television shows. Maybe even a *National Geographic* special. His name would be mentioned in paleontology textbooks. And he'd finally erase his humiliation.

"We need to talk."

His pleasant dream vanished at the sound of Cameron Reynolds's voice. Jake stood from where he'd crouched over the dig and scowled at the other man. "I have nothing to say to you. I told you to stay away from my dig."

"I'll give you back your eggs and tell you who's been sabotaging your dig if you cut me in on the action here."

"I have even more eggs here."

"I've had a look at what was taken. It's another dinosaur altogether. A therizinosaur."

Jake frowned. These eggs were sauropods. "Therizinosaur eggs that big?" He didn't bother to hide his skepticism. But his heart gave a blip in his chest. If this was true, it could be huge. Therizinosaur eggs were extremely rare and no one really knew what they looked like full grown. If he could find an adult skeleton . . . He couldn't even finish the thought. It was too huge to take in.

"I know, I couldn't believe it, either. But it's true." He pulled a snapshot from his shirt pocket. "Take a look."

The snapshot showed a curled dinosaur embryo. It might be a therizinosaur. "Where did you get this?" He didn't give the picture back to Cameron.

"I had one of the eggs run through a CT scanner. I can take you to the rest of them."

"You had something to do with their disappearance—I knew it."

Cameron shrugged. "Okay, maybe I did. But I've had second thoughts. This is too big for either of us alone. We need each other, Jake. You need me."

Maybe he could use help, but it wouldn't be Cameron's. "You could take the other eggs and claim the discovery for yourself. It makes no sense you'd want to join forces."

Cameron's smile looked forced. "I would if I thought I could get away with it. But you've got Kimball here. His word and yours will outweigh mine. But I want in on the discovery." His expression grew grim and determined.

Jake wanted to throw Cameron off the site, but the remote possibility that the man might be right kept him silent. Though everything in him rebelled at the thought of sharing the limelight with this sleazeball, he wanted those eggs.

He gritted his teeth. "Looks like I don't have a choice."

Cameron's uncertain look faded and he grinned. "Don't look so pained. We used to be friends, Jake."

"I'd as soon welcome a cobra into my tent," Jake snapped. "We'll work together, Reynolds, but don't expect things to ever be like they were before."

Cameron's grin faded. "I'm sorry we can't be friends, Jake. I miss the old camaraderie."

Jake did, too, but he wasn't about to tell Cameron that. "Now where are the eggs?"

Cameron glanced at his watch. "Meet me at the turnoff to Milly Pike at nine tonight. We need to go in after dark."

"I want to go now. I'll get the sheriff and get my property back."

"You can't do that." Cameron's voice rose. "If my partner gets wind of it, those eggs will be gone. Do it my way for once."

"Looks like I don't have a choice." Jake folded his arms over his chest. "Now get out of here and let me work."

"I'm part of this now, remember? I'll give you a hand."

"Not until you prove yourself by getting me those

eggs." Jake wasn't going to budge on this one.

Cameron frowned, then shrugged and went toward the path. "Fine. But you'd better get rid of that chip on your shoulder. We've got a lot of work ahead of us."

The self-satisfaction in Cameron's voice as he said "us" made Jake grit his teeth. The last thing he wanted was to share the limelight with the man, but Cameron held all the cards since he was holding the eggs hostage.

He didn't reply and the other paleontologist went down the path to the parking lot, and Jake heard his truck start up and the crunch of gravel under the tires.

He bent back to his work. Maybe Kimball would have an idea of how to get out of this snafu.

Skye stood looking at the Mitchell tube. "How much longer, Pop?"

"Maybe tomorrow we can get the first extraction going."

"That soon?"

"We've been working day and night on this. You realize Peter will get wind of it any minute, don't you? If he shuts us down before we can prove anything to your mother, we're sunk."

"I don't think so." Skye was surprised her mother hadn't told Peter what she was up to.

"I hope you're right."

Skye hoped so, too. "I can't believe Peter hasn't heard about it yet."

"I wish there was some way to keep him busy and make sure he doesn't show up here unexpectedly."

Skye laughed. "He's a real pussycat and here we are acting like we're scared to death of him. He might get upset and go silent for a few days at home, but when we find something, he'll be gung-ho, too. He hired that assayer a few weeks back to see if there was any chance we'd find diamonds. He's wanted this dream right along with us."

James grinned. "You're right. I forgot about that. He'll be on board right away. I've always thought it was admirable the way he has looked out for you and your mom. He gets a little overzealous about it at times, but that's understandable after what you've all been through."

Skye's heart softened at the reminder. "He likes to protect us. I feel guilty I didn't tell him what I was using the money for. I'm thinking about confessing."

"Wait until tomorrow," James advised. "Let's see what the first extraction shows."

"Okay. I'd like to be the one to tell him. It will hurt him less."

James nodded, but she could tell his thoughts were far from worrying about Peter's feelings. "I'll be back in the morning to help with the start-up."

"Sounds good. I'll get back to work and make sure we're ready." James pressed her shoulder then trotted down the tunnel toward his office.

Skye smiled as she watched him go. He was the closest thing she had to a father, closer even than Peter. She didn't know what she'd do without him.

She hurried out into the sunshine. Becca had called

131

this morning and invited her to come to lunch at Windigo Manor. At first, Skye had wanted to turn it down. The last thing she wanted was to run into Jake. But Becca said Wynne was bored and wanted a fresh face in the house.

She saw Jake's SUV in the parking lot and paused in the sunshine to look up the slope of the mountain toward the dig. The path disappeared at the top of the hill, and she couldn't see Jake's head, though a curl of smoke rose above the mountain peak. Maybe it was just as well she didn't see him. What would she say to him if she ran into him anyway? Better to avoid him. At least he was here and not at the Manor.

She started the truck and turned out onto the road toward town. She downshifted and the truck hit a pothole and slewed sideways. As the undercarriage thumped, she heard something from behind the seat. A funny rattle like something loose. She concentrated on the road then jumped when the noise came again. She'd check it out when she got to Windigo Manor.

It sounded as though something moved under her seat. Probably something rolling around. She glanced down at the floorboard and froze. A long, slithery brown snake marked with lighter grayish brown stripes moved from under the seat. It turned and looked at her, and the tongue flickered out.

Skye froze, her hands gripping the steering wheel in a tight clasp. The truck veered toward the right from her spasm. Barely breathing, she righted the truck but didn't dare tromp on the brake. The accelerator felt like a sponge under her foot. She tried to ease up on it, but her limbs felt frozen.

More of the snake's body slithered from under her seat, and it coiled right under her right ankle. She could see the rattle. A timber rattler. Just like those out at Tallulah's. They weren't native to this area, so how did this one get here? She was afraid to breathe, afraid to move.

The truck hurtled along. Skye knew a hairpin curve lay ahead. There was no way she could negotiate it at this speed. Ever so slightly, she eased up on the accelerator. Her instincts told her to get out of the truck, but how? The snake would bite her if she moved.

She swallowed, and her throat made a clicking sound that the snake heard. It raised its head, and the tongue flicked out again. Skye wanted to throw up. Her eyes felt dry and gritty. She blinked rapidly to moisten them. Her muscles felt tight, and her mind raced frantically through her options.

Slowly, slowly, she eased up further on the accelerator. Maybe she could let the truck glide to a stop. She didn't want to go into Higley curve up ahead. The snake might be thrown against her bare ankle. Why had she worn shorts today? If only she had put on a thick pair of jeans and her boots this morning. Now there would be nothing to impede the snake's bite.

The truck hit a bump, and the snake hissed and coiled tighter, its rattle sounding loud in the enclosed space. Skye's breath came in pants. The snake's head was inches from her ankle. Her palms felt slick, and she fought to hang on to the wheel.

She hated snakes and could barely stand to look at it coiled so close. Panic clawed at her chest, but she didn't dare react.

The truck slowed further. With one hand on the wheel, she slipped her right hand over to the handbag on the seat. She opened the flap and eased her fingers inside, searching for her cell phone. There it was. She teased it out with gentle movements then flipped it on its back so the keypad lay upward.

Who should she call? Jake would be the closest—he was only three miles behind her at the mine parking lot. Fortunately his cell number was in her phone from the last time he'd called her. She called it up then pressed Send and brought the phone to her ear.

It seemed an eternity before it began to ring, then it rang four times. Five. She was about to give up when the phone clicked in her ear.

"Jake Baxter."

"Jake, it's me." She whispered in the phone.

"Skye? What's wrong?"

"There's a snake in the truck with me. A timber rattler. It's right under my feet. I'm almost to Higley curve. I can't put my foot on the brake."

"Keep easing off the accelerator."

"I am but the truck is still rolling." Panic rose in her chest.

"Shhh, don't speak so loudly. You don't want to startle the snake. Keep letting up on the gas. But slowly so it doesn't see any movement. Is it coiled and rattling?"

"Yes," she whispered. She let up on the gas some more, and the rattle increased. "It's getting mad."

"I'm on my way, don't hang up."

She heard the sound of an engine start through the phone and closed her eyes briefly. Jake would be here soon.

"You still there?"

"I'm here," she said, her eyes darting from the snake and back to the road. "The truck is almost stopped. Just before the curve."

"Good. Keep it up. Try to let it roll to a stop."

The vehicle barely moved along, and Skye guided it to the side of the road where it finally slowed then stopped.

"I've stopped," she whispered. She could hear gravel hitting the undercarriage of Jake's car. He must be flying along the road.

"Good. Now slowly open your door."

She hadn't thought of that. With her left hand, she reached over and pulled on the door handle. At the noise, the snake's rattle came again, and her gaze darted back to the reptile. It had moved closer to her leg and was nearly touching her. If those scales came in contact with her skin, she wouldn't be able to help herself. She would have to move and would likely be bitten.

She prayed for strength and began to push the door open. Slowly, so slowly, the door creaked open. She closed her eyes. She couldn't watch that snake's black eyes any longer. It was going to bite her, she knew it. A scream built in her throat as she began to lose control.

Her leg twitched from the strain of holding it in one position.

"Skye, talk to me."

Jake's urgent voice calmed her, and she let her breath out. "I'm here. The door is open, Jake."

"What's the snake doing now?"

Skye peeked one eye open, then both eyelids flew open and she stared at the floor. The snake's coil had loosened, and its head turned toward the open door. "It sees the open door."

"Good. Don't move. I'm almost there. I've been driving ninety miles an hour."

Skye glanced in the rearview mirror and saw the SUV kicking up dust behind it as it barreled toward her. The tension in her chest began to loosen. "I see you."

Keeping her eyes on the mirror helped her ignore the danger that lay at her feet. She glanced down, though she didn't want to. The snake had moved toward the open door.

Was it a myth that a snake wouldn't bite unless it was in a coiled position? Skye had never studied the matter. She normally couldn't even bear to look at pictures of snakes. The up-close-and-personal brush with a poisonous one had been almost more than her nerves could bear.

From the corner of her eye, she could see Jake still coming behind her. He still had the cell phone to his ear. "It's moving out," she whispered.

"Good. Hold quiet."

With safety so close, it was all Skye could do to stay

frozen in one position. Her muscles were beginning to ache from the tension, and she wanted to swing her legs to the seat.

The snake's head had reached the open door. Its tongue flicked in and out again as it hesitated. *Please leave. Go.* Skye silently urged its progress.

Swinging its head down, the snake began to slither out the open door. In seconds the last tip of rattle at the end of its body slipped over the floorboard. With a cry, Skye jerked the door shut and jerked her legs onto the seat. Cowering against the smooth leather, she dropped the cell phone and buried her face in her hands, then burst into tears.

Her vision darkened, and she fought the faintness. She wouldn't pass out now. It seemed as though she sat that way for years, then she heard gravel flying and looked into the rearview mirror to see Jake's SUV sliding to a stop. Jake jumped out and stood back as the snake slithered past him and into the grass on the other side of the road.

Jake sprang to the door of the truck and opened it. "Are you okay? Did it bite you?"

"I don't think so but I'm not sure. I'm numb." Tears continued to roll down her cheeks, and she struggled to breathe.

Jake took her hand and helped her from the truck. "Let me see." He knelt on the gravel and ran his hands over her ankles. "I don't see anything."

She could hear the relief in his voice. He stood and pulled a bandana from his pocket then awkwardly wiped her face with it. "Don't cry. You're okay. I can't believe how brave you were. You really kept your head. If you'd panicked and moved, it would have bitten you. God answers prayer after all."

She raised her head at his ironic tone. "You prayed?"

He nodded. "God hasn't answered many prayers for me lately, but He came through on this one."

"I didn't think you were a Christian. You'd seemed kind of cynical."

"It's been hard to trust Him after He let my parents be murdered." His eyes narrowed to slits, and he looked away. "I'd have to say I'm a Christian who's mad at God."

Talking about something other than the snake was calming her nerves. "God never promised us we wouldn't see sin and pain in this life."

"I know. I'm beginning to understand that. I became a Christian when I was fifteen. It was great until my parents died." He sighed. "I've been going to church again."

"I've noticed."

"I've noticed you noticing." He grinned.

Her face burned, and she looked away. At least she knew he was a Christian. If he continued to look at her like that, she would throw herself against his chest. She swallowed hard. "How do you think that thing got in there?"

"Are they common here?"

She shook her head. "We have no native poisonous snakes."

"What about Tallulah?"

Skye's eyes widened. "Could she hate me that much?"

"I'm going to find out," Jake said grimly.

Chapter Eleven

Jake had rushed out of the site so quickly, he hadn't notified anyone of his departure. He had Skye put her head between her legs then called Joe and asked him to keep a lookout on the dig. He then called Kimball and told him to go ahead and he'd be back as soon as he could. He also told Kimball about Cameron's admittance that he had stolen the eggs and what they were. Kimball had whistled when he heard the news, then told Jake to be careful.

Jake hurried back to Skye. He wasn't about to leave Skye while she was in such a state. Her wide, shocked eyes had stared out of a face so paper-white, he'd wondered if she was going to faint. His teasing banter had brought the color back to her cheeks.

He grabbed the canteen at his waist and handed it to her. "Drink," he commanded.

She took a swig and grimaced, but more color came back to her face. "I can't believe even Tallulah would do such a thing," she said. "You think maybe a snake just escaped?"

"How? You remember how she acted. She seemed a nutcase. You never know what people like that will do."

She closed her eyes briefly, and he watched the way her eyelids fluttered. The delicate tracery of veins in her lids made her seem fragile and vulnerable. He wanted to kiss away her fear. The thought made him take a step back. She wouldn't welcome his caress, she'd made that much clear.

Skye opened her eyes and sighed. "Can I go with you to see her?"

"I'll drive." He took her elbow and guided her back to his SUV. "Your truck is far enough off the road for now. I'll call Max and have him and Becca come get it."

"Becca! I'm supposed to be going there for lunch."

"I'll tell her what happened." Jake dialed his cell phone and explained the recent events. He soothed his sister's alarm, and she promised to take care of Skye's truck.

"The keys are in it," he informed Becca before ending the call.

"I wish I'd caught that snake," he told Skye.

She shuddered. "I'm glad it's gone."

"I could have taken it to Tallulah as if I were returning it. She might have been startled enough to reveal something."

"Better you than me. *I* don't want to ever see it again." She clasped her arms around herself and stared out the SUV's window as he sped toward Tallulah's place.

"We've got to plan our strategy with her. Just coming in and accusing her will get us nowhere. I think I'll have a look at her snake building." He tried to remember how many snakes had been in there. She'd said a hundred, he thought. One by the door had been particularly large.

"Count me out." The look of distaste on her face made him smile.

"They're caged. They can't hurt you. But you can stay outside while I check it out."

"Maybe we'll be lucky, and she'll be gone."

"Fat chance. But we'll handle whatever happens."

"Should we call the sheriff?"

"I'll drive and you call him, though he doesn't seem eager to solve this one."

The road was empty of traffic. He pulled the SUV to the side of the road and parked at the road. No reason to announce their presence by driving into the lane. "You up for a hike?"

"Do I have any choice?"

"You can stay here until I get back." He knew she'd never agree. And in truth, he was half afraid to leave her alone.

"I'll come." She unfastened her seat belt and got out.

He stared at her critically. "You're still pretty pale. Maybe you'd better wait for me."

"I'm fine." Her voice was defiant. "Let's get going."

"It's quite a hike to her house," he warned.

"I know that better than you."

"You're getting feisty. That's a good sign." He grinned and she scowled at him. "Those flimsy sandals aren't much good for hiking." He pointed to her feet.

"I can outrun you any day." Her chin lifted, and she stared him down.

He held up his hands. "Truce. Why are you mad at me?"

The fire faded from her eyes. "Sorry. It's not your fault." She looked tired.

"No, it's not. If I remember correctly, *you* called *me* to come to your aid. Rescue the damsel in distress." He was beginning to think he wanted to be more to her than just a strong body to call when she was in trouble.

"Oh, shut up." Her eyes sparked again, and spots of color sprang to her cheeks.

He grinned. "Let's go, Sleeping Beauty, before I get in more trouble." He took her hand, and they stepped into the forest. She tried to tug her fingers loose, but he held on to them and she seemed to relent, curling them into his. He liked the feel of her small hand in his. It felt natural, though that intimate gesture was a rare one for him.

Skye also seemed content as they walked through banks of wildflowers, and as he helped her hop over streams. The scent of pine sprang from the needles crushed under their feet. The forest was alive with movement.

Skye flinched and leaned against him when a garter snake slithered past her sandals. "Steady," he said soothingly. He ran his hand along her long braid as she pressed her face against his chest. His pulse kicked up a notch. He liked the feel of her thick braid, silky and heavy in his hand. Why did holding her always feel like it was what he was meant to do?

He didn't want to linger on this attraction to her, didn't want to spend the long hours between dusk and dawn thinking about her. She haunted his dreams, and he didn't like it. Maybe he needed to buy one of her dreamcatchers.

He released her, and she stepped back.

"Sorry," she said, rubbing her eyes. "Let's get this over with."

He nodded and started through the woods again, but this time, he let her find her own way. The more distance between them, the better for his peace of mind.

The ground sloped away before them, and the small structure lay at the bottom of the hill. The place looked deserted. Maybe this would be easier than it looked. Slipping and sliding, they made their way down the steep incline.

At the edge of the clearing, he pointed to a boulder thrusting up through the ground. "Wait there," he whispered. "I'll see if anyone is around."

"Her bicycle is gone."

He glanced around and nodded. "Good. But wait here anyway. Can you whistle?"

She nodded and pursed her lips. She warbled like a songbird.

"Great. Do that if you see her come."

"Be careful." Her dark, doelike eyes were anxious.

Before he could help himself, he bent and kissed her quickly. A reassuring caress was what he'd intended, but he wasn't prepared for the shock it caused in him.

How did she do that? He pulled away and took off toward the snake house. He didn't dare look in her eyes and see the distaste he was sure was there.

The padlock was firmly fastened. He grimaced. If he broke it, Tallulah would know someone had been here. But so what? They'd be long gone, and if he could find proof for the sheriff, it wouldn't matter. He went around behind the house and found a crowbar hanging on a hook by the back door. Perfect.

The padlock resisted his efforts at first then broke free with a clang that echoed through the forest. He jerked the door open and went inside. The smell of dirty cages hit him first. He looked around at the cages filled with snakes. Several reptiles hissed and struck at the glass that separated them.

He glanced around the room. One of the cages was empty. If he remembered right, it had held a large timber rattler last time they were here, though the fact it was empty was no proof the snake had been put in Skye's truck. The dirty wooden floor felt springy beneath his feet, as if it was rotten as he went to the far wall where a desk was shoved in the corner.

He sat in the attendant rickety chair while the snakes rattled and moved through the cages behind him. He pulled open the first drawer but all he found were records of the sale of venom to a lab in Detroit. The second drawer held bank transactions. He switched to the other side. Nothing.

He stood and went toward the door, suddenly noticing a shrill whistle that had grown in decibels. Skye had been whistling for several minutes, and he just now realized it. He sprang for the door, his sudden movement riling the snakes even more.

He gained the exit and saw a movement from the corner of his eye. Tallulah was bicycling along the lane. She seemed oblivious to his presence, and he stepped to the side of the snake building and hurried around the back of the house. Creeping through the edge of the forest, he joined Skye where she crouched behind the boulder.

"I thought I was going to have to come get you," she whispered.

"Let's get out of here." He grabbed her hand, and they ran for the deep woods. They'd just gained the top of the hill when he heard Tallulah shriek. She'd evidently discovered her padlock broken.

"Hurry!" Skye pulled at his hand. "If she gets more snakes out, I'll freak."

"Me, too. Some of those suckers were huge." He panted as he ran. It was harder running up the hill than it had been going down. Tallulah was screaming imprecations into the wind.

They reached the edge of the forest and stepped onto the road. "She had to have noticed the SUV," Jake said.

"But she might not know who owns it."

"She could find out. Not that I'm afraid of her."

She paused to catch her breath. "I looked around the yard and found a rattlesnake totem in the yard."

"What does that mean?"

"It means she looks to the rattlesnake to protect her

and to give her vindication from her enemies. So she might have used one to try to hurt me." She opened the passenger door and got in. "There's more. Look." She held out a long feather. "I found it in an unlocked shed."

"So?"

"So, it's my father's. The one missing from the box of his belongings."

"So she took it after all."

"There were other things there. All kinds of power fetishes." She shivered. "Let's get out of here before she comes back."

The sheriff listened to Skye and Jake relate what had happened. "It's pretty thin evidence." Sheriff Mitchell shook his head. "Lots of Ojibwa have totems in their yards. And snakes can and do escape. There's no proof it was deliberate." He picked up the feather. "How do you know this is your dad's? It just looks like an eagle feather to me."

"I know the feather. I looked at it every day. Trust me."

"Okay." He sighed heavily. "I'll have another talk with her."

Skye rolled her eyes at Jake as the sheriff left the manor. They'd both known he wouldn't move fast on this. At least they were out of that horrible woman's hideaway. She shuddered just thinking about it again. Her gaze went across the living room of Windigo Manor and met Wynne's.

Wynne frowned. "You're not drinking your tea, Skye.

You've had a scare today." She turned to Molly. "Hey, pumpkin, would you ask Moxie to bring some cookies in, too?"

"Sure." Molly hopped down from the sofa where she'd been sitting beside Skye. "Don't worry, Skye. Uncle Jake will protect you."

Skye managed a smile, though her gaze wandered to Jake. He stood talking to Kimball by the doorway. They were deep in discussion about the eggs again. She leaned her head against the back of the sofa and closed her eyes. Fatigue weighted her eyelids and made her muscles ache. She wished she could crawl in a bed somewhere and forget about this day.

Especially the memory of the kiss. Why did he persist in doing that? Was he trying to drive her crazy? She would never forget the way he'd sprang to her rescue today, like a knight in shining armor. Like Indiana Jones himself. She opened her eyes and watched him.

His floppy hat was in his hand, and she could see the shaggy hair that was usually covered. Thick as a thatched roof, it was nearly as dark as her own. A tan line ran across his forehead from the constant hat on his head, and stubble darkened his jaw. His bronzed muscular arms were shown to advantage in the old T-shirt he wore. He was every inch a man.

If only he would quit doing such sweet things, she could resist him. Though he was inordinately handsome, for her the real attraction lay in the way he cared for his family and the strength of character he showed in everything he did. Skye wished he would take his eggs and go somewhere else so she could rediscover the contentment she'd had before his appearance.

Jake must have sensed her eyes on him because his gaze rose and caught her own. Their eyes locked and he gave a slight smile that made her stomach plunge. He was her enemy. She had to remember that. She was so close to finding the diamonds, and now that he'd found those eggs, he would shut her down. There was no way they could both win. If it came to a showdown, she knew her mine would be the one to pay the price.

He smiled, and she found herself smiling back though she wished she could glare instead. Kimball said something and Jake followed him out of the room, much to Skye's relief.

"My brother likes you, you know," Wynne said in a soft voice.

Skye froze. How did she answer that? "He's a nice man," she said, wincing inside. Nice was such an insipid word for a man like Jake Baxter.

Wynne smiled. "Nice? I've never heard him described that way. Intense, focused, but not nice. You must have it bad, too."

Skye felt the heat rise to her cheeks. "I don't know what you mean."

"You can't keep your eyes off him. And he's the same way. It's like watching two magnets try to avoid one another." Wynne laughed, but there was kindness in it.

"He's not the settling down kind."

"And you're not the type to go with him? Is that what you're saying?"

"No, I'm not. I will never leave Eagle Island."

"Never is a long time. Don't you ever want to travel? Life with Jake would never be boring."

"It's not like he's breaking down my door, you know," Skye pointed out.

"He would if you gave him some encouragement."

"It's not just his wandering though." Skye leaned toward Wynne. "He's told me he's a Christian, but he seems to be struggling with God right now. I can't let myself love someone who doesn't share my faith."

"Ah." Wynne nodded. "I'd hoped you would lead him in the right direction."

"I don't think it should work that way. I've seen too many people end up marrying someone whose faith is weak thinking the person will grow stronger eventually. There are always problems with that."

"Jake is a good man." Wynne sounded defensive.

"I'm not saying he isn't, but that's not enough." Skye swallowed. She'd revealed more than she wanted. Not that it would have mattered about the relationship since she wasn't going anywhere and Jake wasn't staying.

"I'm going to start working on him," Wynne said. "I've just prayed and not said much but that's wrong. I know the problem is our parents' deaths. I thought he'd come to grips with it on his own, but I have a responsibility to talk to him."

"He's got a hard head."

"Don't I know it!" Wynne shook her head. "And if I'm honest, the real reason I've never talked to him about it is he's my big brother. I've always held him in a little bit of awe, and I've been leery of having him upset with me. We're close and I've been hesitant to do anything that might damage that." She sighed. "It's hard to admit I'm a coward."

"I think most of us are when it comes to our family."

Wynne glanced into Skye's face. "It's hard to imagine you being frightened of anything."

"You should have seen me with the snake today." Skye could smile about it now but it hadn't been funny then. "Maybe Becca can help you with Jake. You both seem to have settled what happened to your parents in your own minds."

"We all went to church when we were growing up, but Jake had a friend who made fun of Christians. It affected how he saw things, I think. And when our parents were killed, he blamed God. He said if God would reward faithful servants like our parents that way, then what benefit is it to follow Him."

Skye winced. "The age-old question—why do bad things happen to good people? Jake said he's beginning to understand. There are no easy answers, though."

"I know, I struggled with it, too. I finally came to the verse in Job that says 'where were you when I formed the world?' Sometimes you just have to realize God is in control and sees things we can't see and acts for purposes we can't know. It's all about trust."

"And trust is hard for people. Especially take-charge people like Jake," Skye agreed. "He's got a strong sense of justice."

She looked away and stared out the window. The

150

darkness outside seemed to crowd in the window, and she wondered if Tallulah was watching her even now.

Jake came to the door. He looked grim. "I've got to go out. I'm going to get back my eggs."

"I'll go with you." Skye stood, though she was almost too tired to think.

"No, you stay here. I won't be gone long."

"I'm coming with you." She rose and started after him.

Chapter Twelve

Jake glowered at Skye sitting across from him in the SUV. "I still think this is too dangerous. Why can't you ever listen to reason?"

"Like you do?"

The eyebrow she quirked made her look a bit like Spock, and he stifled a grin. He liked her spirit. In fact, he liked most things about her. Unfortunately.

He dragged his gaze from her knowing grin and concentrated on the road.

"Do you really think you can trust Cameron?"

She echoed his own misgivings. "I don't have much choice if I want to get those eggs back." He turned down River Road as Cameron had instructed.

"I wish you'd told the sheriff."

"Cameron was adamant about that. We have to play this his way." Jake saw Cameron's truck parked at the side of the road ahead. "There he is."

"There's nothing out here but deserted mine shacks and a large tract of forest."

"And my eggs," Jake said grimly. And he would have them back tonight.

He pulled behind Cameron's truck, and they got out. He went to the truck window and peered in. "He's not here."

He turned and squinted through the darkness. "I don't know where to look. He said he'd meet me here."

"Call him," Skye suggested.

Jake felt a reluctance to announce their presence so plainly. The trees crowded close to the road, their branches seeming to reach for him and Skye, a hungry yearning that unnerved him. Rustles and night sounds from the darkness of the deep woods whispered to him. An owl hooted, and Skye jumped. Jake shuffled uneasily.

"Stay here," he said. "I'll take a look around."

"I'd rather come with you." Her voice sounded hushed and strained.

Jake had to wonder if Cameron was doing this to unsettle him. If so, Jake would show him he hadn't succeeded. He walked past the truck and along the dirt road.

He wondered if anyone ever came back here. It had a desolate feel. Cameron had to have chosen this spot on purpose.

The flashlight in his hand pushed back only the edges of the inky darkness. Maybe he should have come out sooner to survey the terrain.

"He doesn't seem to be here. Is there a cabin or house in the woods near here?"

"There's an abandoned miner's shack just off the road here. But no one has lived there in decades."

"Show me." He handed her the flashlight.

After a hesitation, she took it. "It won't be easy. The ground is pretty rough. Stay close."

The last thing he wanted to do was get separated in the darkness. "You can count on it."

Shining the light on the ground, Skye led him into the deep woods. Pine, oak, birch and maple trees crowded close together so thickly it was hard to push through. Brambles tore at his clothes in the darkness. He wished he'd insisted Cameron meet him in the daylight. This was ridiculous.

Skye stumbled and fell, and the flashlight flew from her hand and landed on the ground. Jake helped her up.

"You okay?"

"I'm fine." She sounded disgusted.

"I'll get the light." He grabbed the flashlight and handed it back to her. "Is it far?"

"Should be just down this slope."

He wanted to hang on to her hand, but he let go and she went ahead of him again.

After struggling through a patch of thorny shrubs that left him with scratches, he saw a patch of moonlight shining on a small structure.

"That it?"

"Yes."

"Doesn't look like Cameron is here." His anger

toward the other paleontologist for bringing him out on this wild-goose chase was growing.

He took the flashlight from Skye and stepped through the clearing to the building. "Cameron?"

He felt like an idiot calling for the other man in the middle of obvious wilderness. There was no one here.

"I'm scared, Jake," Skye said in a small voice. "Something doesn't feel right."

He felt it, too. A prickling along his neck and back. Probably just animals watching them, he told himself.

"Let me check the shack, and we'll get out of here." It wouldn't be too soon for Jake.

His flashlight swept the old miner's shack and came to rest on something near the door inside.

"What's that?" Skye's voice was hushed.

Jake didn't answer, but he went closer. She stayed right on his heels.

He focused the beam on the object, and his fingers tightened on the flashlight. The yellow glow settled on Cameron's face. From the shape of his head, Jake knew he was dead. Someone had crushed his skull.

Skye uttered a small shriek, and he put his arm around her.

"I'd better call the sheriff."

A movement caught his attention, and they turned to see Wilson running away from the cabin.

The sheriff's department had rigged bright lights around the scene, but the unnatural illumination failed to reassure Skye. She watched Jake talk to the sheriff.

He stood with a stillness that added to the seriousness of the situation.

Murder. The thought made her vision glaze over. It seemed so incongruous on her small island. Her throat constricted. She'd liked the paleontologist, in spite of Jake's animosity.

Jake. Skye's gaze was drawn to him again. Would he be a suspect? He'd made no effort to hide his dislike of Cameron.

She clasped her arms around herself and joined the sheriff and Jake.

"When was the last time you saw the deceased?" Sheriff Mitchell asked.

"This morning," Jake said, taking Skye's hand.

She curled her fingers around his palm. Maybe she could bring him some comfort. She knew he had nothing to do with this, but she knew how strangers were regarded with suspicion in the small, insular community. The sheriff might not be so quick to discount Jake's involvement.

"You say you were supposed to meet him at the road. What made you look here?"

Skye could hear the suspicion in the sheriff's voice, and her stomach tightened.

"He was nowhere around, so we started looking in the area."

"And I remembered the shack," Skye put in.

The sheriff ignored her. "Did you call out?"

"Not until we got to this shack."

Now that the sheriff had asked, it had been odd that

Jake hadn't called out for Cameron at the road. Skye glanced up at him. That would have been the logical thing to do. And she'd even suggested he do it.

"Why did you search here?"

"I told him about this miner's shack," Skye said again.

The sheriff's glance quelled her, but she stared back at him with a challenge in her eyes.

"Please let Mr. Baxter answer, Skye," Sheriff Mitchell said.

Skye gave a slight nod, but she narrowed her eyes at him to let him know she wouldn't stand by and watch him railroad Jake.

"So Ms. Blackbird told you about this place, and you decided to come here. Doesn't that seem odd to you when he was supposed to meet you at the road? What if he came back while you were gone? Maybe he'd just stepped into the forest to relieve himself."

"Maybe so, but I was impatient to find him."

"Why were you meeting?"

"He was going to help me recover something that had been stolen."

The sheriff raised his eyebrows. "Stolen goods? Why wasn't I informed?"

"He insisted we not call you in. My first inclination was to notify you."

Sheriff Mitchell scribbled in his notebook. "I hear you and the deceased didn't get along. Did you kill him, Mr. Baxter?"

"No."

156

Jake's quiet denial held the ring of truth, and Skye hoped the sheriff recognized it.

"But it's true you disliked him?"

"That part's true enough," Jake admitted.

"It sounds to me like you had good cause for wanting him dead. You believed he'd taken something that belonged to you. From what you say, he was basically blackmailing you into letting him take part in your project."

"It wasn't like that. I could have refused."

"But you didn't. Maybe you lured him out here and hit him over the head with that shovel. It was an easy way to get rid of him."

Skye couldn't keep quiet any longer. "Then why bring me out here to find Cameron? Why not let the animals take care of the body? No one would have missed him for a long time."

The sheriff pursed his lips. "He still didn't have the eggs back, right? Maybe he hoped this man's death would serve as a warning to whoever else is involved."

Skye was finding it harder and harder to contain her anger. "Sheriff, you need to find the murderer instead of harassing Jake. You're barking up the wrong tree." She hesitated. She hated to drag Wilson into this, but it had to be done. "We saw Wilson New Moon running away from the cabin, too."

The sheriff flexed his jaw. "Why didn't you say so before?"

"Wilson wouldn't hurt anyone, but he might have seen something."

"I'll ask him." The sheriff put away his notepad. "When the coroner determines time of death, we'll have more to go on. Wilson may shed some light on things. And he's a strange one. He might have done it himself." The sheriff tipped his hat and left them to go talk to two of his deputies.

"Let's get out of here." Jake led her back to the road, and they stumbled up the ditch to the SUV.

Skye felt tainted and dirty from the experience in the woods as she settled into the passenger seat and fastened her seat belt.

"And I still don't have my eggs back." Jake sounded resigned.

"Is that all you care about? Don't you care that a man is dead?" Skye frowned at his callousness.

He shrugged. "I'm not going to be a hypocrite and pretend to be upset. Cameron was a blight on humanity. It's too bad he's dead, but he tended to run with some unsavory characters. He basically admitted he had an accomplice. This was just a way to get them back to me and ensure he got a piece of the action. We have to figure out who his accomplice was. That's the murderer."

"I can't imagine who could be involved on our island. No one here would be interested in your eggs."

"I thought from the start it had to be Cameron. No one else here cared about the eggs. But someone else does. And whoever it was killed Cameron. "

The web around her seemed to be growing more complex. "We're going to have to figure this out. It's obvious the sheriff likes you for the murder. He didn't even seem too interested in talking to Wilson."

Jake nodded. "Let's go over what we know." He ticked the details off on his fingers. "You were attacked at the mine, the eggs were stolen, and someone lobbed rocks at you."

"Or you could have been the target in that as well."

He nodded. "Okay, one of us or both of us were attacked with rocks. Someone put a rattler in your truck, Cameron offered to lead me to the thief and he was killed."

"They don't seem to be related," Skye said. It seemed hopeless. Maybe there were two separate things going on.

"Everything seems to spiral back to the mine," Jake said, rubbing his chin. "Tell me a little about its history."

"Its history?" Skye frowned. "It's been in my family since the eighteen hundreds. The garnets found here have been some of the largest and most beautiful in the country. Its production has slowed in the last two decades though. My father was always convinced there were diamonds in there, too, something that occurs occasionally in a garnet mine."

"What if there really are diamonds there and someone knows it?"

"You mean they want to prevent me from finding the diamonds?"

"What if they want to close the mine down, discourage you from keeping the mine open? Maybe they're hoping to be able to buy it once it's closed and they can have the diamonds for themselves."

"But who?"

"Your stepfather or mother?" Jake suggested.

Skye tensed. "Don't be ridiculous! My mother would never do anything to hurt me. Peter is quite happy to let the garnet mine wander along. Besides, if the diamonds were found, the money would be his and Mother's, not mine. I only want to find them to fulfill my father's dream not for the money."

Jake let out a huff of exasperation. "Then who? Tallulah wouldn't have the money to buy the mine, and I can't imagine someone like her having that kind of ambition. She seems content to raise her snakes in her little cabin in the woods."

Skye nodded. "Nothing makes sense."

"We've got to figure it out, or I may be making a trip to Superior Penitentiary."

"But how?" The task seemed monumental to Skye. "And how could the dig be involved?"

"If there really are diamonds in the mine, our perpetrator wouldn't want me messing up his extraction once he's in possession of the mine."

"That's true."

"How far are you from finding diamonds?"

"We're about to start the extraction process in the Mitchell tube. James plans to start it up tomorrow."

James. Could he or her cousin Michael Blackbird want the mine for their own? The idea seemed preposterous to Skye, and she pushed it away.

160

"So things may be heating up at the mine. We need to watch the comings and goings there closely. Maybe it's a worker, or even someone in town with the money and drive to gain the mine. The new casino will be finished soon. It could even be an organized crime group that's associated with the casino."

Skye nodded. "There have been a lot of strangers coming and going lately. I'd like to believe it's someone like that rather than someone I know." She shivered. Could there be such darkness behind the smiling face of one of her friends?

"What about Tallulah?" Skye asked. "How does she fit in?"

"Maybe she doesn't. Maybe she's just someone who hates you."

Skye sighed. "You mean more than one person wants to hurt me? I've tried to reach out to everyone I know, to be a friend. I can't imagine who else I would have offended."

Jake leaned over and squeezed her hand. "We'll figure it out."

Skye's cell phone rang, and she rooted in her purse for it. She was afraid it was about to click over to voice mail but she finally managed to dig it out and punch the button. "Skye Blackbird."

"Skye, you need to get to the mine." James's voice sounded strained. "There's been an explosion."

Chapter Thirteen

The stars shone in the night sky like a million of those elusive diamonds against a backdrop of black velvet. If only the diamonds in Skye's mine were as plentiful and as easily seen. Skye rubbed the gooseflesh on her arms, cold more from James's words than from the temperature.

Explosion. Every mine owner's worst nightmare.

She should call her mother and Peter, but she dreaded hearing how this was all her fault for pressing into the Mitchell tube, for she had no doubt that was where the explosion had occurred. Her stomach twisted at the thought of what she might find. She just prayed there were no fatalities, no injuries.

They usually didn't work the miners at night, but James had been having round-the-clock shifts since he wanted to have some kind of proof to show Peter, who would eventually find out how Skye had used the loan money from the bank.

"Is there anyone I can call for you?" Jake asked, breaking into Skye's thoughts.

She glanced across the seat at him. He'd insisted on driving her out to the mine, and he'd kept his foot buried in the accelerator. They were coming up on the mine now—in record time. Skye wasn't sure she was ready to see what was waiting at the end of the road.

"No, I'll have to call my mother and Peter."

"You make it sound like the end of the world."

"It might be the end of my managing the mine," she admitted. "Mother has never been sure it's a job for a woman anyway. She just might yank it from me."

"It might not be that bad. Maybe it's just a small explosion that did no real damage."

She shook her head. "James sounded grim. It's probably worse than I imagine." The scent of smoke came through her open window, and she grimaced. "Smell that? I wish we could see something." She moved restlessly on the seat.

"We're almost there." He managed one last hairpin curve and pulled into the parking lot.

Skye was out the door almost before he brought the SUV to a stop. She took off for the mine at a dead run. Jake was on her heels. The spotlights and the bright moon illuminated the smoke billowing from the mouth of the mine. She felt sick at the sight.

James stood talking with two other men near the mine door. Skye recognized them as the second shift foreman Willy and her cousin Michael.

James saw her as she ran toward them. "It's bad, Skye."

He didn't have to tell her—she could see it by the way the smoke billowed from the opening. Only his eyes peered from a face blackened by smoke. "Is everyone okay, Pop?"

"Yes, no injuries."

She closed her eyes. "Thank You, God," she whispered. She opened her eyes and stared at him. "The Mitchell tube?"

He nodded. "Yep. What little progress we'd made is gone. That whole corridor is buried in rubble." He rubbed his chin and sighed.

"What about the rest of the mine?"

"Fine. Nothing else was touched."

Michael was looking worried. "If I didn't know better—" He broke off and looked away.

"If you didn't know better?" she prompted.

"I'd say it was deliberate."

Jake arrived to hear Michael's comment. "You think someone used an explosive?"

Her cousin shrugged. "It was powerful—not like a cave-in. I can't imagine what else would have caused it."

Skye absorbed the information in silence. The thought had flickered on the edges of her conscious thought all the way out here, she realized. Hardly anyone knew what she was doing, though. Who would have wanted to stop the exploration?

She turned to James. "What do you think, Pop?"

"I think it was just an explosion of gas or a cave-in. But Michael knows more about it than I do."

She wished she could believe it was a spark that ignited gases in the mine. She had a sinking feeling it was more than that. "Could it have been a disgruntled worker?"

"Maybe." James sounded weary.

"When can we get in to assess the damage?" Jake asked.

"Probably morning. The dust and smoke are still settling."

"What can cause an explosion like this?" Jake stepped nearer to the mine entrance and peered in.

"A spark can ignite gases in the mine," Skye told him.

"But you don't think that's the cause of this one?"

"I'm sure beyond a doubt. But Michael has a different view." James glanced toward the other man.

Michael shrugged. "Maybe I want to believe it was sabotage rather than negligence. I thought we were being extra careful."

"You were." Skye held her watch up to the light. "Let's all get some rest. Maybe it will look better in the morning."

"Maybe," James said in a monotone.

She could tell by James's tone of voice that he didn't believe a word she said. His pessimism fueled her feelings of inadequacy. Maybe this was her fault. "We're lucky no one was hurt. That's the important thing."

Michael nodded. "Luckily, it was break time and everyone was outside eating their dinner."

James took off his filthy hat and rubbed his head. "It could have been worse. We had ten men down that corridor earlier in the evening."

"Well, send them all home. We'll deal with this tomorrow." She glanced at Jake. "Could you run me to my mother's?"

"You're going to tell them?" James asked.

"I have to tell them tonight before they hear it from somewhere else."

"Too late," Jake said, his gaze going past her to the parking lot.

She turned to see Peter and her mother getting out of the car. Skye wasn't ready for this. How did she tell Peter she'd taken the bank's loan and put it in the mine? He'd kill her. She swallowed hard and turned to greet them.

"Skye, are you all right?" Her mother reached for her.

Skye burrowed against her mother's shoulder. The comfort of the embrace was what Skye needed right now. She felt she'd been reeling from blow after blow for days. Tears welled in her eyes, but she held them back. The last thing she needed was to show weakness in front of the men. And in front of her mother. She had to prove she was competent to stay in charge of the mine.

Even if she wondered about that herself.

Forcing a confidence to her voice that she didn't feel, she pulled away. "I'm fine and so is everyone else."

Her mother patted Skye's face. "That's all that matters then. I know you, Skye. You're probably running through a thousand scenarios to see what you could have done differently, but you stop it right now. These things happen sometimes. It's no one's fault. And it's certainly not yours."

Peter patted Skye on the shoulder. "We'll get it back up in no time, Skye. Don't fret about it."

The comfort in his voice brought her even closer to tears. "I was going to tell you about this today anyway, but there's something you don't know."

Peter raised an eyebrow. "You sound scared. You should know by now not to be afraid of me."

"I just don't want to lose your respect," she whispered.

"You won't. What is it?"

"I didn't use the loan money on The Sleeping Turtle. I used it on the mine."

For a minute his face was impassive, then the beginnings of a frown flickered between his eyes. "Why didn't you tell me in the first place the mine needed some capital? I would have given you money toward it. You wouldn't have had to borrow money for that. I thought we were in this together."

"I knew you disapproved of what I wanted to do."

His face slackened, and his jaw dropped open. "Don't tell me you opened the Mitchell tube!" He glanced back toward the mine opening where dust still billowed.

"Yes," she admitted in a small voice. "I did."

"And that's where the cave-in occurred?"

She rushed on at his clipped voice. "Michael thinks it might have been deliberate."

"That's ridiculous. I told you the Mitchell tube was dangerous!"

"I think we should assess things before blame is thrown around." Jake moved out of the shadows.

"I suppose you encouraged her in this," Peter said, scowling at Jake.

Skye's mother put her hand on her husband's arm. "Remember your blood pressure, Peter." She turned her gaze to Skye. "We should have told him. I was wrong to keep it from him."

"I know, Mother," Skye said meekly. "I was going to

tell him today, but everything started happening."

Peter's jaw twitched. "You knew about this, Mary? Why didn't you tell me?"

"You'd always said the Mitchell tube was dangerous. I didn't want to worry you."

"And I was right." He sighed and his voice softened. "There's no help for it, I suppose. We'll have to live with the consequences. How extensive is the damage?"

"James says the rest of the mine is fine, but the Mitchell corridor has caved in."

"Just as well," Peter said. "Maybe now you'll listen to sense." His face softened as he looked at Skye. "You're young, Skye. I know the impetuosity of youth. We all have to take our licks and learn the hard way. I'm sure you'll listen now when you're told an area is dangerous. And no one was hurt, so things will be fine."

A wave of love for her stepfather swept over her. He might scold her, but he always supported her in the end. "Thanks, Peter. I'm sorry I disappointed you."

"We'll talk about it tomorrow," her mother said. She leaned up and kissed Skye's cheek. "I'm going home to bed. This is too much excitement for me." She tugged on her husband's arm. "Come along, Peter."

Peter pressed her arm. "You get to bed, too, Skye. You look done in."

Skye watched them walk away and let her breath out.

"That wasn't as bad as you thought it would be, was it?" Jake fell into step beside her as she headed for the SUV.

"No, it wasn't. But there may be more coming."

"I'm going to poke around a little in the morning. Just in case you're right about it being sabotage. I'm not an expert, but I've dealt with my share of people tampering with my digs. I might turn up something."

Trails of dust still blew in wisps from the mine opening. It was early, only seven. Jake stared at the mine entrance. He could do this. The last time in there he'd been upset about Skye being injured. There was no such problem today.

In spite of his silent encouragement to himself, he paused at the door into the mine. He hated closed-in spaces. That was one reason he loved his job, loved living out under the stars. No walls pressing around him, threatening to squeeze the breath out of his body.

He hated to let a childhood incident rule his adult life, but no matter how many times he told himself he would stride forth into a tight place, his throat would close up and his chest would squeeze until he was gasping for breath.

But today was a new day. He was going to walk through that door and explore the cause of the explosion. And no petty fear of close spaces was going to have him running. Flexing the muscles in his jaw, he strode forward.

A new wave of dust and smoke hit his lungs, and he coughed, sweeping his hand back and forth to clear the air so he could see. His chest tightened, but he ignored it. Moving forward with his hand on the rough stone wall, he went in the direction of the sounds he heard:

men talking and the sound of equipment.

The hallway sloped downward, and Jake paused, fighting the tightness in his chest. *I can do this*. He took a couple of deep breaths, coughing when the dust expanded in his lungs. His chest squeezed even more.

Michael materialized from an opening on the right. "Jake, can you come here a minute? I need someone to hold a light." He beckoned with his hand.

Swallowing his rising nausea, Jake focused on following the other man. All he had to do was put one step in front of the other. Easy as falling into the water. This was not a problem.

Keeping his gaze on Michael's back, he went down the side corridor. Was it his imagination that it narrowed as he went along? Jake told himself not to gauge it, not to watch the walls.

Michael was crouching in the rubble at the end of the corridor and rubbing his hands over some marks on the wall. "Focus the light here. I want to take some pictures."

Glad to be able to concentrate on something other than the way his chest felt every breath and every beat of his heart, Jake knelt on one knee and aimed the light. He looked at the way the rock was gouged out and rubbed his fingers against the black.

"Looks like an explosive." He brought his hand to his nose. "Smells like it to. You need to get an explosive expert in there. I'd say there's a distinct possibility this explosion wasn't an accident."

"That's what I thought all along," Michael said

grimly. "I was taking every precaution on this project, and it wasn't unsafe."

"Have you told Skye?"

"No, I was trying to keep her out of this. She won't be happy about it."

"But it might get rid of some of that guilt she's carrying around."

"You don't know the half of it. That girl carries the world on her shoulders."

"Any idea why?" Jake stood and resisted the urge to bolt for the door behind him.

"She thinks it's her fault her father left, and she's been trying to make it up to her mom ever since."

"Why would she think that? It's always about the adults, not the kids."

"She and her dad—my uncle—had an argument the night he left and she told him she hated him and to stay out of her life."

"That hardly sounds like Skye. She seemed to adore her dad."

"She did, generally. But at that time, she was wanting to open The Sleeping Turtle, and Uncle Harry wanted her to come to work with him at the mine. They argued about it. She didn't mean a word of it, but Skye can be pretty hotheaded."

"I've noticed." Beads of sweat had popped out on Jake's forehead. He pulled out his bandana and wiped them away. "So with him gone, she's all the more determined to do both."

"Exactly. I've told her she's going to kill herself

trying to do everything, but I have to admit she's doing a fine job of both professions. But she doesn't have a social life." Michael looked at Jake with a sly grin. "Until you came along. You've been good for her."

Jake's pulse blipped. He told himself it was from the tight space, but he knew he was kidding himself. Skye was coming to mean more to him than he liked. "She's an interesting woman."

Michael laughed. "I've seen that look in a man's eyes before—I've had it myself. You're caught, man, and you know it." He leaned against the wall of the tunnel. "I've always believed God puts us in the orbit of the one person who will fill in that missing piece of ourselves. Watching you and Skye together, I'd say those pieces fit about as well as any I've seen."

"Funny, you don't look like a romantic." Jake grinned and mopped at his forehead again.

"You can laugh if you want, but we'll see who's laughing this time next year when you've got a ring on your finger."

Caught. Trapped. The words meant the same thing to Jake. Skye meant to shackle him to this tiny island. His claustrophobia came over him again in a wave, and he turned and bolted for the door.

Chapter Fourteen

The sheriff tipped his hat. "Sorry to bother you, Skye, but I have a few more questions. Busy night last night for you, I hear."

"In more ways than one." Skye gave the swing she sat in a little shove and leaned into the movement. Gulls cawed above her head and dove into Superior's waves just offshore. She wanted to forget the day before, forget a man had been murdered and the mine had suffered an explosion.

She felt battered by circumstances, hollow with shock. The last thing she wanted was to answer more questions. But there was no choice. Heaving a sigh, she dug the toe of her sandal into the soft dirt to stop her swing. She got up from the swing and followed the sheriff to the gazebo by the giant sycamore tree.

This spot behind her cottage had been her refuge since she moved here three years ago, and it felt tainted by the sheriff's presence. He'd brought the troubles with him. She couldn't hide here any longer.

He took out his notebook. "How well do you know Jake Baxter? I've heard in town that you're sweet on one another."

The blandness of his tone softened the shock of his hidden accusation for a minute, then she gasped. "What are you trying to say, sheriff?"

"You're together when you find Jake's enemy. Now how does that look when I find out you're sweet on him? I'll tell you—it looks like you're covering for him. But why? That's what I want to know."

Skye wanted to shout, but she forced herself to speak calmly. "You're way off mark, sheriff. I barely knew Cameron. Do you have a time of death yet?"

"Yep. Yesterday afternoon around three. Where were you and Jake then?"

Three. That was before she'd shown up at the dig, before the snake incident. Jake had been there at four when she showed up, but she couldn't vouch for how long he'd been at the site. Surely he had an alibi though.

"I was at the store," she said finally. "You'll have to ask Jake about his whereabouts."

"Oh, I will." The sheriff capped his pen and put it back in his pocket with his notepad. "One more thing, Skye. I wondered if you knew he threatened Cameron?"

"Threatened him how?" The sick feeling in the pit of her stomach wouldn't go away.

"Said he'd kill him if he double-crossed him again. What if Cameron did just that? Would you still protect Jake if you knew he was a murderer? I don't want to stir up trouble for the Baxters, but Cameron was pretty persuasive. I have to check it out, now that he's dead."

"He's not a murderer, sheriff. Talk to anyone. He's a highly respected member of the scientific community."

"Even well-respected people commit murder, Skye. Or leave their families, or do any one of the things they shouldn't."

She winced at the reference to her father. "That was low," she muttered.

He shrugged. "Maybe. But you need to wake up and throw away those rose-colored glasses. We have a murderer on the island. Cameron was bludgeoned to death. Someone hit him at least twenty times in the head with that shovel. That shows true viciousness. I'd hate for you to get in that person's way."

"Then find him! Or her. Have you talked to Tallulah yet?"

He shook his head. "I've got more important things to do than chase down a half-demented woman. She's not our murderer."

"What about Wilson?" Skye's voice rose, and she gulped. She had to stay calm or Mitchell would dismiss her as a hysterical female.

"I haven't found him yet, but he's still high on my list of suspects, too." He tipped his hat and walked across the lawn, then disappeared around the side of the cottage.

Skye bit her lip. She needed to talk to Jake. Pausing long enough to grab her handbag, she fumbled for her keys and raced to the truck. She drove along the roads as fast as she dared.

The entrance to the mine was blackened. The violence of the explosion looked out of place when the rest of the hillside slope was covered with vegetation and flowers. Jake's SUV was in the parking lot and she glanced up the path to the right of the mine opening that led to Jake's dig. She got out of her truck. Maybe she'd check with James first about the explosion. There might be some news about that.

As she neared the entrance to the mine, she saw a movement from the corner of her eye. Jake was leaning against the mine door.

He pulled his canteen from his belt and took a swig then saw her. "Good morning."

"Did you find anything?"

He nodded. "Looks like an explosion was set off. I told James to call an explosives expert, though maybe the sheriff will do that."

"That might shake up his preconceived certainties." She told him about Sheriff Mitchell's visit this morning.

He was shaking his head as she talked. "Sounds like I need to contact a lawyer. He'll be coming for me any time."

"We have to figure out who the real killer is," she said.

"So you don't think I did it?"

"Of course not! And I don't think Sheriff Mitchell does, either. He's a little lost on where to look." She lifted her chin in the air, and her gaze caught his. She spiraled down into the tenderness in his dark eyes. His fingers grazed her chin, and he bent his head.

She took a step back and gave a shaky laugh. "You rattle me too much, Jake. I need to keep my distance."

"I think I'm the one being rattled," he said softly. "You're right though. Thanks for the reminder."

His face was impassive once again, and if she didn't know better, she would have sworn there had never been the yearning she'd glimpsed in his face. "So where do we start?"

Jake rubbed his chin. Skye noticed the dark stubble along his jawline and wondered if he'd even gone home to bed. He looked weary.

"Cameron had an assistant—Brook Sawyer."

"I've seen her around town." Skye nodded. The young woman seemed to idolize Cameron. "Let's go talk to her. Any idea where we might find her?"

"Maybe she'll be at his dig packing things up." He nodded around the other side of the mountain.

"You want me to drive?"

"I'll do it." He dug his keys out of his pocket and led her to the SUV. They drove around the access road to the other side of Turtle Mountain. "There she is," he said, nodding toward a lone figure carrying a backpack to a gray midsize car that was parked just off the road.

He pulled the SUV behind the car, and they got out as a young woman of about twenty-five arrived at the automobile. Her wispy blond hair was pulled back in a ponytail, and dark circles shadowed her blue eyes. Thin almost to the point of gauntness, she had sinewy muscles along her legs and arms.

Her gaze darted from Skye to Jake and back again. "What are you doing here?" She dropped the backpack and stood with arms folded across her chest. "Don't you think you've done enough?"

"I'm sorry about Cameron." Jake's tone was mild.

Brook blinked but maintained her belligerent stance.

"I'll bet. You hated him, and now he's gone." Her voice was thick, and her eyes filled.

Jake sighed. "I didn't hate him. I didn't like some of the things he did, but we'd been friends once and I didn't want to see him hurt."

"Did you kill him?" Brook thrust out her jaw.

"No. But I want to find out who did. Don't you want that, too?"

"Yes."

"Then help us figure it out. He asked me to meet him out there. He said he knew who took the eggs. Do you know anything about that?"

Brook glanced from Jake to Skye. "Maybe."

"Then tell me."

"You just want your eggs back."

"I won't lie and say I don't want to recover the eggs, but I want to find out who killed Cameron, too."

"If I help you, will you make sure he's recognized for his aid in the recovery?"

"Don't blackmail us," Skye put in. She could empathize with the young woman, but she was growing tired of the manipulation.

Brook threw up her hands. "This isn't blackmail! But, whatever, I'll help you."

Sky softened her tone. "Sorry. We need your help. If you want to find Cameron's killer, you'll help us. Do you know who took the eggs?" Skye thought maybe Brook would be more apt to answer her questions than Jake's. The animosity she felt toward Jake was palpable.

"No, but I know Cameron met with the person several times."

"Man or woman?" Skye still thought Tallulah was the most likely culprit, and she kept remembering Wilson's babble about the Spider Woman.

"I never saw the person except from a distance. I couldn't tell if it was male or female, though the person was only a little shorter than Cameron."

Tallulah was as tall as many men. Skye pressed her questions. "Where did they meet? Maybe we can track down the eggs that way."

"There's another old miner's shack deeper in the woods behind the one where he was killed. Near the east side of Turtle Mountain. They met there."

"So that person probably killed him," Skye said.

"Maybe."

"Did you tell the sheriff this?" Skye asked.

"No."

"Why not? Don't you want Cameron's killer found?"

"The sheriff only asked me about Jake's relationship with Cameron. I didn't think about it at the time." Brook rubbed her forehead. "I was too upset to think. I suppose I should tell him."

"I think we'll run out and see what we can find while you tell the sheriff what you know," Skye said.

Jake had never been this deep into the North Woods. The lack of noises of civilization was a little unnerving. No drone of cars, no hum of machinery, no human voices.

"Kind of far in, aren't we?" He paused to wipe his forehead. The taste of insect repellent was bitter on his tongue. The buzz of insects around his head comforted him in the absence of other noises.

"We're almost there."

"Have you been out here before?"

Skye nodded. "I've been all over the island in my search for herbs and roots. I don't come here much, though."

"Why not?"

"It was my dad's favorite place to hike. It hurts too much to remember all our walks through here."

"You want to go back? I can go alone." He'd thought she looked a little pale, but he'd thought it was because she was tired.

"No, I'm fine." She brushed past him and continued along the path. "This trail has been an Ojibwa hunting trail for centuries. It leads back to the mountain to a sacred site where our ancestors prayed and began the hunt every spring."

"Did you come here often with your dad?" Maybe it would help her to talk about it.

She nodded. "Nearly every week. Most of what I know about herbs and roots I learned from him. His mother, my grandmother Eloise, was the tribe's medicine woman and she taught my father everything she knew."

"And he passed it on to you."

"Yes." She fell silent then pointed ahead. "There's a clearing through that brush where the old miner's cabin sits." She picked up her pace and plunged through the tangle of overgrowth.

Jake followed. The brambles tore at his clothing as though they wanted to stop his advance. He felt a high sense of adventure. Maybe the answer to all their questions would finally be found here. He was tired of being in the dark. He wrenched past one last tug of thorns and entered the clearing. Skye stood staring at a lean-to that was nearly covered over with vines and brush.

"That's it? Why would they meet there?"

She shrugged. "It's remote and a fairly easy place to find since the trail leads right here."

"Who all knows about this trail?"

"Any Ojibwa knows."

"You think the murderer would be Ojibwa then?" He said the words with a bit of caution. He didn't want to put words in her mouth.

She bit her lip. "Most islanders don't wander the woods in this area. It's part of the Ojibwa reservation. I can't imagine any of my people who would do this."

"What about Wilson New Moon?"

"Oh, no, he wouldn't hurt anyone."

"Could he have seen something here? He's still hiding out somewhere, right? Something scared him."

"I'd forgotten about that," she admitted. "I should try to find him and bring him here, see if he saw anything."

"I'm probably grasping at straws," Jake said. He was too tired to think clearly. At least Brook would tell the sheriff what she knew, and maybe Mitchell would get off Jake's case.

She smiled. "Maybe." Skye walked toward the lean-to. Kneeling down, she scanned the ground.

Jake joined her. "My dad was a master at finding things in the woods. He could spot mushrooms everyone else just walked right past."

"What's this?" She reached for a key on a key ring. It was still shiny so it hadn't been out here long. The key had a dot of blue paint on it.

"What kind of key is it?"

"It looks like a car key." She turned it over and looked at the key ring. "From Turtle Bank."

"That's your stepfather's bank, isn't it?"

She nodded, and he thought she paled.

"Does it look familiar to you? You look funny," he said.

Her fingers closed around the key. "It could belong to anyone. Peter gives these out to all the customers."

"Tell me what you're thinking."

She frowned. "It looks like my cousin's key. See this dot of paint on it? He uses it to differentiate between keys." She pointed to the smear of blue.

"Why would Michael be out here?"

"I don't know. Maybe he was mushroom hunting." She stood and brushed twigs from her slacks. "Let's look around a little more." She moved toward the lean-to and went around behind it.

There was something she wasn't telling him, but he could tell by her manner that she wouldn't say anything more. He followed her. Just behind the lean-to, the ground sloped upward into the mountain. A hole in the mountain was nearly overgrown with brush.

"What's that?" He pointed to the opening.

"An old mine shaft. I think it leads into the Mitchell tube eventually. My dad always wanted to explore this side of the mountain, but the access was a problem."

"You ever been in there?" Not that he wanted to explore it. His stomach churned at the thought.

"No, my dad would never let me. It's been abandoned for decades and isn't safe."

As Jake turned around, he saw a shadow flit from tree to tree. "Hey, you there!"

Skye whirled to look, too. "Wilson, I want to talk to you."

Wilson's moon-shaped face poked from behind the tree, then he jerked around and took off.

"Come back!" Skye took off after Wilson. He raced along the path as if a demon were after him.

Skye was soon panting from the thick humidity. Jake ran with her.

"I'll catch him!" He accelerated past her toward Wilson's bulky figure.

Chapter Fifteen

Skye caught up with Wilson and Jake at the edge of the clearing. Wilson had been running for all he was worth, and Jake tackled him from behind. Jake gave her no chance to do more than gasp as he caught Wilson by the arm and lifted him to his feet.

"What were you doing spying on us?" Jake demanded.

The whites of Wilson's eyes rolled up, and he shook like the aspen leaves above their heads. "I didn't do nothing," he said. His lips trembled.

Skye grabbed Jake's arm. "Let him go. He won't run, will you, Wilson?"

The man shook his head. "What do you want?"

Jake let go of Wilson's arm, but he continued to stare at him with wariness in his manner. "We want to ask you some questions."

Wilson stood rubbing his arm. He shuffled from one foot to the other. "I don't know nothing."

"Do you come here often?" Skye used her most gentle tone. Wilson was terrified enough, and she didn't want to upset him any further.

The man nodded. "It's my place."

Jake opened his mouth, but Skye quelled him with a look. "Do you ever see anyone else here?" she asked Wilson.

He nodded. "Sometimes." He ducked his head and didn't look her in the eye.

"Anyone you know?"

"Maybe." He looked crafty.

"Have you seen Cameron Reynolds here?" Jake burst out.

"Let me handle it," Skye hissed.

Jake subsided with an impatient huff.

Wilson stood with his mouth agape and a distant expression on his face. "I don't know no Cameron."

"He digs in the ground," Skye prompted.

"Like *him*," Wilson said.

"Yes, like Jake here. You were at the cabin last night. Someone hurt him."

"I didn't see nothing." Wilson shrank away.

They'd better change the subject or they would lose him, Skye thought. "He was trying to find eggs. Have you seen any rock eggs, Wilson?"

He nodded. "Seen lots of them."

"Where?" Jake put in. His rising voice betrayed his eagerness.

Wilson shrank back. "There," he said, stretching out his arm.

Skye turned to look with Jake toward where Wilson indicated. The man was pointing at the entrance to the old mine shaft. "In the mine?"

Jake paled. Skye's stomach sank. She didn't want to go in there, either. "We'll tell the sheriff," she said.

"The Spider Woman put them in there. She was pretending to be a man, though."

"What man?" Jake and Skye said in unison.

"When did you see her put the eggs in there, Wilson?" Jake asked.

"Sometime." Wilson looked vaguely off to the side. "Before the dark man came."

"Does he mean Kimball?" Jake asked.

"The dark man who digs in the ground with Jake?" Skye asked.

Wilson nodded. "Before that. It was night, and the Spider Woman brought them."

"The Spider Woman or a man?"

"They're the same," Wilson said, confusion clouding his eyes.

"Okay, how do you know the Spider Woman is a man?" Jake asked.

Wilson shook his head in confusion. "He was bad. He hit the other man with the shovel. Bam, bam!" Wilson pantomimed with his hands as though he held a club. "He whacked him again and again until he didn't move anymore. Then he ran away."

Skye licked her dry lips. "You're sure it was a man."

"He was tall. Big as a house. Big like Spider Woman."

Skye suppressed a sigh. Wilson was rambling.

"I want to go home now," Wilson announced. "I saw your daddy, Skye."

Her heart kicked. "When, Wilson?"

"When he came here." He waved toward the mountain.

"Lately?"

Wilson took a step back. "I need to sleep now." His expression took on a stubborn cast as he settled beneath the tree and pulled his hat over his eyes.

Frustration rose in her chest. "Now what?" She was afraid to hope he knew what he was talking about. Could her father have come back?

"Maybe he'll talk more later. We should take him to town for the sheriff to talk to him." He gave her a kind look. "Don't go getting your hopes up that your father has come back. Time is murky for Wilson. He was likely talking about sometime in the past before your father went away."

"Probably," Skye admitted. "But what if Wilson saw him recently?"

"Don't go there." He squeezed her shoulder. "We need to let the sheriff handle Wilson."

"You think you can carry him for half a mile through heavy forest?" She nodded to the big man lying on the ground.

"We'll get the sheriff out here." He pulled out his cell phone and looked at the screen. "No signal."

"I'm not surprised. What if one of us goes for the sheriff, and the other one stays here to watch Wilson." She knew what he would say before he answered. Typical male.

"You go."

"No, I'd better stay here with Wilson. He'll be scared if he wakes up and sees you."

"Like the sheriff would listen to me."

He had a point. "Maybe you're right." She glanced at Wilson again. "He might sleep until I get back."

"You might be able to get a signal at the road and just call the sheriff. Then you could come right back here to wait on him."

"Okay. Try not to scare him if he wakes up."

Jake touched her hand. "Be careful. I think you need these." He tossed her the keys to the SUV.

She caught it midair. "I'll be back as soon as I can."

The hum of the bees through the wildflowers in the

meadow made Jake wish he could take a nap himself. He settled on a rock and waited. As he jiggled his foot, he kept glancing at the opening. If only he could make himself go in there to look. He stood and walked closer.

The opening was only about four feet in diameter. No way could he crawl in there. He wished there was someway to get over this paralyzing fear. Skye said God didn't give a spirit of fear, but of power and a sound mind. He puzzled over what she meant. He'd been watching her, and if God was what made her different from most women he met, that extra something was intriguing. It made him long for something unnamed, something that almost frightened him.

A total reliance on God.

His chest squeezed at the thought. He knew he was God's child, but Jake liked control. Giving it up to someone else, even God, was too difficult.

But maybe it was necessary for true happiness. He pinched the bridge of his nose with his fingers. "Are you listening, God?" he said the words tentatively, as if the Creator might actually answer.

Out here in the wilderness, he could almost feel the Lord nearby. He was probably just tired today, or he wouldn't be thinking like this. He hadn't been to bed last night at all. He heard the sound of someone tromping through the woods and turned to look. Kimball Washington batted a branch out of the way and stepped into the clearing.

"What are you doing out here?" Jake asked, going to meet him.

"I ran into Skye on her way to find the sheriff, and she asked me to come keep you company."

"She couldn't get him on the cell?"

Kimball shook his head. "Her cell phone was dead."

"I should have given her mine."

"She said she'd be back as soon as she could." Kimball looked toward Wilson, still sleeping beneath the tree. "Maybe we should take another crack at asking him questions. Skye told me what was going on."

"Let's leave it until the sheriff gets here."

Kimball raised an eyebrow, his gaze sweeping Jake's face. "You look done in. Why don't you take a nap yourself?"

"I wouldn't be able to sleep a wink. Not knowing those eggs may be in that tunnel." He pointed out the spot to Kimball.

"I'm not going in there. God gives us common sense for a reason."

Jake arched his eyebrows. He'd never heard Kimball talk about God before. "I never knew you were a Christian."

"Last time we met I wasn't." Kimball settled on the rock beside Jake. "I finally 'saw the light,' as they say." He grinned.

"I have to say I'm surprised."

"Why?"

"You're a man of science. Some say they don't go together."

Kimball's smile widened. "Do you believe in dinosaurs, Jake?"

189

"Of course." Jake wondered if Kimball had been in the sun too long.

"Why?"

"I've found their fossils." Where was Kimball going with all this? Jake moved impatiently.

"But you've never seen one."

"I've seen the evidence they existed."

"And the evidence God exists is all around us. You believe in dinosaurs because you see the bones, but how do you explain the way all the stars maintain their orbits, the way the ocean tides move in and out. And what about the beauty all around us? There is an Intelligent Designer, Jake. There has to be."

"Hmm, I've never really thought about that. I believe in God because I believe. It's that simple and that hard. I hadn't thought about hard evidence." What Kimball said made sense. Jake looked around with new eyes. Every word the man said strengthened Jake's sleeping faith.

Kimball went on. "Science says it's survival of the fittest. Man is defenseless, yet he rules the world. Does that make sense?"

"I guess not." Jake stretched his legs out in the sun. "Didn't it feel weird to give up control to God? I've never done that, despite my faith. I've always held on to that last little piece."

"Yeah, it felt a little weird. But you know what—it was a relief, too. I sure wasn't doing that great a job running my own life. I figured I didn't have anything to lose by letting God have a shot at it. You might give it a try."

Jake tried to stifle the longing in his heart, but it came back in a resurging wave. He'd always admired Kimball more than any other man. And Wynne and Becca had that same sense of peace that Skye had. That contentment was missing from Jake's life. What Kimball was saying made a lot of sense. But no, not yet.

His chest closed up. "Not now. I'll think about it. Maybe I'll go to church with the family on Sunday." It was all very well and good to say he wanted to give God control, but he didn't see how he could do it. What if God asked him to give up paleontology?

"Don't wait too long," Kimball warned. "When the Holy Spirit is calling to a course of action, it's never wise to turn away."

He didn't want to be a nut about it. Did he? Maybe he did. He hadn't done a great job of running his own life. Sure, he'd had success in his career, but it hadn't erased the emptiness in his heart.

"You've gone off the deep end," Jake said, forcing a laugh.

"The water's refreshing here," Kimball said with a cheeky grin. He clapped his hand on Jake's arm. "I'll be praying for you, buddy."

"I appreciate it." Jake stood and stretched his legs. "The sheriff and Skye should be back anytime."

Kimball cocked his head. "I thought I heard something."

A distant rustle came to Jake's ears. "Me, too." Unease touched him. The sounds seemed stealthy. Skye and the sheriff wouldn't be trying to mask their steps.

Something whistled by Jake's head and plowed into the ground by Wilson. "Get down!" He threw himself to the ground. "Someone's shooting at us."

Another bullet plowed into the tree above Wilson's head. The big man jumped to his feet and crashed into the forest. "The Spider Woman!" Running as if a swarm of bees were after him, he disappeared into the thick brush.

Jake started to get up to go after him, but another bullet zinged by overhead. "Where's the sheriff when you need him?"

"I'll circle around and try to catch him. Keep him occupied." Kimball belly-crawled toward a downed tree.

"Be careful!" Jake hissed. He jumped to his feet and ran toward a boulder, then hit the dirt as another bullet flew past his head. The guy seemed to be coming closer. Jake couldn't quite tell what position the shooter held.

Picking up a rock, he tossed it into a rocky outcropping. Nothing. Crouching, he ran toward a nearby tree. He felt a burning on his left arm and looked down to see a thin trickle of blood on his forearm where a bullet had nicked him, probably the one that seemed to have been aimed at Wilson.

He charged toward another rock, but no bullets greeted his movement. Where was Kimball? A roar echoed from the forest, and he squinted to see Kimball charging toward three white birch trees that grew together. Jake jumped to his feet and rushed to help.

Kimball's war cry had faded when the two men came face-to-face. Jake looked around. "Did you see anyone?"

Kimball shook his head. "He was shooting from here though—look." He pointed to bullet casings on the ground.

Jake started to pick one up, but Kimball stopped him. "This is a job for the sheriff."

"At least he won't be able to deny someone shot at us."

"Unless he says these are old bullets."

"He'll believe you," Jake said. "But why would someone want to shoot Wilson?"

"Unless Wilson knew too much?"

"We've got to find out what he knows," Jake said grimly.

Chapter Sixteen

"Not much we can do tonight." The sheriff peered through the darkness at the ground. "The shooter is gone, and so is Wilson. I'll see if I can track him down tomorrow."

"He'll corroborate the fact we were shot at," Jake said. He hoped the man wouldn't talk nonsense. If he started spouting about the Spider Woman, the sheriff wouldn't listen to a word he said.

"You're hurt!" Skye pointed to the dried blood on Jake's arm.

Reaching into her purse, she pulled out an ointment and took his arm in her hand. The touch of her fingers took the sting out of the wound. He smelled some woodsy scent in her hair from the herbal shampoo she used. Her ministrations were so typical of who she was—a nurturer through and through.

He loved her. The realization nearly rocked him on his heels. The emotion had crept up on him when he least expected it. His life felt like it was spiraling out of control. Out of his control, at least.

That realization made him step back from her. "I'm fine. We can look at it later."

Kimball fell into step beside them as they followed the sheriff's light out of the forest. Jake knew Skye had to be tired because he was exhausted himself. It was nearly three in the morning. Maybe these feelings he had were a result of his fatigue.

Glancing at Skye walking beside him, he knew he was kidding himself. He loved everything about her. Her intensity and courage, her caring for other people, the tiny lines between her eyes when she was determined.

But shackling himself to this island was another story. He realized it was all about control again. If he married Skye, he wouldn't be in control of his own life—he would have to take her needs and wants into consideration. Maybe he wasn't ready for that any more than he was ready to give control to God.

Skye stumbled, and Jake grabbed her arm and helped her through the underbrush. The moon was gone, and the woods were black and sinister. Good thing the sheriff had a flashlight. His own had given out.

Skye was visibly drooping by the time they found the road. Jake opened the SUV's passenger door for her, and she practically fell into the seat. The wound on his arm was beginning to throb.

He told Kimball he'd see him later and rounded the back of the SUV. "We're all worse for the wear," he said, slinging his rangy form under the wheel. "I'll have you home in no time. Your mom is going to kill me for putting you in danger."

"I think it was the other way around." She leaned her head back against the headrest. "Besides, she thinks you can do no wrong."

"And what does her daughter think?" Jake would have grabbed back the words if he'd had the chance. He stared straight ahead at his headlights probing the darkness of the night. He'd never fished for a compliment before in his life.

"She thinks you're pretty wonderful, too," Skye said after a long pause. "In fact, she'd like you to come to dinner tomorrow."

His chest expanded, and he no longer felt the sting of the bullet wound on his arm. "Good, I'll be there." He would have said more, but he glanced over to find her head lolling to the side and her eyes closed.

She was asleep. The tension eased in his muscles, and he smiled. They had time to explore this new relationship, or whatever this was.

Unless he turned tail and ran for his life.

Skye barely remembered stumbling into the house and into her bed. The noonday sun drove shards of light behind her lids by the time she awoke. The thought of what Wilson had said about her father came back to her mind. The rational part of her mind knew she was grasping at straws but she had to check it out.

She jumped into her clothes, then cleaned the house and did the laundry. She'd talk to her mother over dinner. Her heart gave a flutter. Jake would be there for the meal. She didn't know how she had gotten up the nerve to invite him, but he'd seemed different last night.

Her smile broadening, Skye grabbed her keys and headed to her truck. "Mother?" Skye stepped into the house and sniffed the aroma from down the hall. Her mother bustled around the kitchen fixing dinner. The aroma of pot roast mingled with that of the apple pie cooling on the rack. Skye should be hungry, but her stomach was too tightly clenched to feel hunger pangs. She didn't want her mother to flip out when she heard the news.

"Oh, Skye." Her mother glanced at her. "Dinner won't be ready for a bit. Are you hungry?"

Skye glanced at her watch. Five o'clock. "No, I got up late and didn't eat until two."

Her mother put down the spoon and turned to face her. She ran a worried gaze over Skye's face and form. "Are you all right?"

"Fine. I was just out late with Jake." She held up her

hand when she saw her mother's countenance brighten. "Investigative work."

Her mother's approving smile faded. "It must have been quite late."

"After three this morning." Skye perched on a bar stool and watched her mother turn back to her preparations. "Um, Mother, I heard something last night. I don't know if it's true or not." She tried to keep the excitement out of her voice, but her mother stopped stirring the gravy and looked at her with a frown between her eyes.

"You look a little flushed. Are you all right?"

"Yes." She looked down at the counter. "Maybe, er, I don't know."

Her mother put down the spoon again. "What is it, Skye? You're scaring me."

Just what she didn't want to do. Skye sighed. "Wilson says he saw my father." She began breaking lettuce into salad bowls.

"Wilson New Moon?"

"Yes. He seemed to know what he was talking about, Mother. Do you know where Father might be hiding out?" It was all she could do to sit calmly on the stool when she wanted to be out searching for her father.

Her mother was shaking her head even before Skye stopped talking. "Skye, this is wishful thinking on your part. Your father is never coming back."

"But what if it's him?" Skye pressed the question. "Wilson doesn't generally lie."

"I know that, but he does get confused. There have

been other times in the past where you thought you saw your father. For your sake, I wish Harry would come back and face all of us, but that's not going to happen."

Skye clung to her hope. Her mother was wrong. This was real. "You don't know that." But her heart sank anyway. She remembered Wilson's words. He wouldn't say he'd seen her father recently.

"I *do* know it and so do you, if you'd admit it." Her mother came to Skye and put her palms on Skye's cheeks. "Let it go, Skye. You can't live your life looking for your father every day. Put it behind you. We have a good life here, don't we?"

"Yes." Skye tried to smile but her lips trembled.

"Peter has taken good care of us. Don't you realize how this hurts him—this continual and obsessive search for your father? Peter has done everything humanly possible to take Harry's place. You keep throwing Peter's love back in his face."

"I don't mean to do that. Peter knows I love and honor him for all he's done for us."

"He doesn't do it for thanks, I don't mean that. But it makes him feel he'll always be second best."

"Mother, Peter came into our lives when I was eighteen. I grew up with a father I loved. No one can take his place. Peter knows that, and he knows he holds a special place in my life. Michael and James try, too, but no one can be a father to me now except my own."

Her mother sighed and her hands dropped to her side. "You're so stubborn, Skye."

Skye dropped her head. Maybe she *was* stubborn, but

198

if there was even a chance . . . "So where might I look for my dad?"

Her mother spread out her hands. "I don't know. Maybe the reservation. His brother might have heard from him."

Skye hadn't talked to her uncle Louis in months. He was a strange man, always going off for months at a time into the deep woods to "meditate and commune with the spirits of the forest" as he put it. She'd have to track him down and see if he'd seen her father.

And while she was at it, she'd see if this key she'd found was Michael's. If his father was at the reservation now, Michael was likely there as well. She pulled out the key. "This look familiar, Mom?"

Her mother picked up the key. "Not really. There are hundreds of them around town."

"I think it might be Michael's. He paints his keys like that. I can check it out when I go out to the reservation."

"Where did you find it?"

"In the meadow where I talked to Wilson."

"You've got one too many salads prepared, Skye," her mother said.

Skye looked down. "Um, didn't I mention I invited a guest for supper tonight?"

"No, you did not." Her mother smiled, a sly grin that made Skye gulp and look away. "The handsome pale-ontologist, right?"

"Jake and I had strategy to plan on how to figure out who killed Cameron."

Her mother's smile faded. "I wish you wouldn't get

involved with that, Skye. It's too dangerous."

"I live for danger." She grinned to show she was kidding, but her mother's sober face didn't lighten.

"I'm not kidding, Daughter."

"I know, Mother. I'm just joking. I'll be fine." She jumped at a knock at the door. "That's probably Jake. I'll get it." She hopped down from the stool and hurried to the door. She swung it open and smiled at Jake.

She was kidding herself to say her heart didn't leap like a deer at the sight of him. His dark hair was still wet from his shower, and his freshly shaven chin made him look especially appealing. Dressed in khakis and a black shirt that deepened the darkness of his eyes and hair, he brought a surge of excitement to the room.

"Am I too early?"

"Nope, you're right on time." She stood aside to allow him to enter. "Peter isn't home from the bank yet, but supper will be ready in about half an hour. We can plan strategy until then."

He held out a bouquet of flowers, and her chest squeezed.

"I brought something for your mother," he said.

The flowers were for her mother. Her pulse settled down to a slow blip again. She should have known better. Jake had made it clear he thought of her only as a friend, even if he'd taken a step in her direction last night. It was foolish for her to wish for something more.

"I'll get a vase for them. Mother loves flowers."

He followed her to the kitchen. "Something smells good."

"Jake brought you flowers, Mother." Skye grabbed a vase from the shelf and filled it with water, then put the flowers in it.

"How sweet of you, Jake! I hope you're hungry."

"Starved, especially after smelling it." He sniffed, and a slow grin spread across his face. "How about you ditch Peter and marry me?"

"Do I hear you making time with my woman?" Peter entered the kitchen. He shook hands with Jake. "You seem to be holding up well. Any news from the sheriff?"

Skye smiled at her stepfather. He never knew a stranger and could put anyone at ease. His presence had added a warmth to the group. She wondered if Peter really liked Jake or if he was pretending for her sake.

She glanced at Jake out of the corner of her eye. What was not to like? Handsome, personable, he exuded a confidence that was compelling.

At least to her. She glanced at her mother and noticed the doting smile on her face. Maybe Jake had that effect on all women.

Jake kept up a steady stream of easygoing conversation, and Skye noticed Peter and her mother relaxing as they all ate. She showed the key to Peter, but he said lots of people did that and he didn't think it meant anything. Jake ate two pieces of apple pie and downed three cups of black coffee before Peter offered to help her mother with dishes.

Skye took Jake to the family room. Minx, the black cat she'd had since she was fifteen, took one look at

Jake and proceeded to climb his pant leg.

He stroked the cat's fur as he settled back against the overstuffed cushions on the sofa. "The sheriff hasn't come looking for me, has he?"

"Nope. Maybe the gun casings were enough to convince him."

Jake nodded. "It's about time." He leaned toward her. "I had an idea."

The suppressed excitement in his voice startled her. "Oh?"

"What if I leave some less valuable eggs out and have Joe off duty so they're unguarded? You could drop me off so there's no vehicle around, and maybe the culprit will take the bait."

Skye didn't like the sound of that. "I don't want you doing it alone though. How about if we park the SUV in a secret spot I know?"

"Okay."

She hadn't thought he would agree. "When do you want to do it?"

"How about tomorrow night? Things will have died down a little. Could you start a rumor around town that I've found something even more exciting? Maybe Joe could tell a few people that he's sick or something."

"News travels fast in a small place like Turtle Town," she agreed. "It might work. Maybe we should draw the sheriff in on it."

"Okay. Before it gets dark so our shooter doesn't see the headlights."

"About six?"

"Great. Meet me at Windigo Manor."

The next morning, Skye parked her old truck in front of the reservation's general store. The building's weathered gray facade looked like it could have been plunked down in a John Wayne Western. She skirted the missing board in the walk and went inside.

Michindoh, the big Ojibwa who ran the store, looked up from arranging pots of thimbleberry jam on the counter. "Hey, Skye. What brings you to the rez?"

"Looking for my uncle Louis, Michindoh. Have you seen him lately?"

"Sure, he just came in from a trip to the wilderness a couple of days ago. I think I saw him going into the casino."

Figures. The only other thing Uncle Louis liked more than the wilderness was a slot machine. She thanked Michindoh and went down the street to the casino.

The glittery building was in sharp contrast to the rest of the sad storefronts. The excitement inside was palpable with the noise of coins being dropped into slot machines and the sounds of players calling to one another at the craps table.

Skye hated the casino. She'd seen the vice of gambling destroy her people with the merciless grip of greed. If she had her way, they would all be swept off Ojibwa land.

She went straight to the slot machines. Her uncle was the only one playing the machines. He sat hunched over a machine near the middle of the bank of one-armed bandits. His long gray braid at the nape of his neck hung nearly to his waist, and he wore a leather vest over faded jeans.

"Hey, Uncle Louis." Skye sat beside him.

He gave her a vacant smile that sharpened when he saw her. "Skye, what brings you out here?" His gaze was drawn back to the slot machine. He scowled. "Stupid machine is rigged."

"Can I talk to you for a few minutes?" she asked.

"Sure." He whacked the machine with the flat of his hand and stood. "Want a pop? We can go to the diner."

"Okay." She followed him out of the casino, breathing in the fresh air with the eagerness of a drowning man coming up for air. The stale cigarette smoke and the stink of booze made her feel dirty.

The diner was empty at ten in the morning. They slid into the red, cracked seats and ordered soft drinks.

"You've got that look on your face," her uncle observed. "You're here for a reason."

She nodded. "Wilson New Moon claims to have seen my dad. I figure if he's around, he would have contacted you. Have you seen him?"

Her uncle's eyes widened, and she didn't think the shock on his face was feigned. "Your father—are you sure?"

"That's what Wilson says."

"I think he's pulling your leg. I've heard no rumors about your dad being back."

She tried to hide her disappointment. "That's what Mother says. But Wilson seemed positive."

"Why would he come back? Your mother married Peter right away. He had to feel betrayed."

"Oh, Uncle Louis, you know that's not true." It was an old argument. "Father had been gone three years before Mother divorced him for desertion. What was she supposed to do—wait the rest of her life for a man who just walked away from his wife and daughter?"

"He would have come back," her uncle said, his jaw thrust out.

"When? It's been eight years. I think if he had any intention of coming back, he would have at least called. He's never even sent a card."

A shadow crossed Uncle Louis's face. "He will. He won't let that mine go." He leaned forward. "How's the extraction going? Any diamonds yet?"

"We had an explosion a few days ago. It caved in the Mitchell tube."

Her uncle winced. "You've got to get it opened, Skye. Your dad knew it was there."

She chose not to answer that. "Where would Father hide out if he decided to come back?"

Uncle Louis rubbed his chin. "Maybe the old tube along Duncan Creek."

"I was out there yesterday. It's all overgrown." Skye frowned as she tried to think of the terrain. The soil was so rocky nothing much grew out that way except brambles so she hadn't had much occasion to hunt for herbs there. Could her uncle be thinking of a different tube along the old mine?

He shrugged. "Your dad was always a dreamer. He

called that his poet cave. He used to go there and write poetry for your mother, for all the good it did him."

"She's never shown me the poetry." Skye wasn't sure about this new side of her father. He'd been so focused on the mine, she never dreamed he was so romantic.

"She probably threw them away."

"I doubt it." Skye had seen other mementoes in the cedar chest in the attic. She'd never delved too deeply into the old chest—it hurt too much.

"Part of that mine belongs to me, you know." Her uncle took a slurp of his soda.

This was an old argument and one that had caused the family to splinter. Michael still pressed the issue, too. "Let's not get into that again." Her shoulders slumped. She wasn't up to this today.

"Your father promised me my half if I worked for him. I worked for him for ten years and never got the first bonus."

"He paid you a good wage."

Her uncle snorted. "Harry promised me diamonds. I don't have so much as a diamond ring for my pinky finger. You've got to find those diamonds, Skye."

"I've been trying. I think my father was just a dreamer, Uncle Louis. If he was so certain they were there, why did he leave?" It was the eternal question that haunted her.

Her uncle studied the bubbles in his soda. "I'm sure he had his reasons."

"Like another woman?" Skye had been wanting to ask that question for years. She didn't dare utter it around her mother, but it would explain a lot.

"Your father worshipped your mother! He never looked at another woman."

"Did he get in trouble with the law?"

"You know how he was always pushing religion down my throat. He'd give himself up for jaywalking."

Skye let out her breath in a huff. "Then why?"

"I don't know."

Her uncle's brows drew together, and she knew he hated having to admit ignorance. Skye drained the last of her pop and stood. "Thanks for the information, Uncle Louis." She stopped and turned. "Hey, does this key belong to Michael?" She pulled the keychain from her purse.

Her uncle stared at it. "Maybe. Want me to give it to him?"

"I'll be seeing him at the mine. I just thought you might know. I thought he might have dropped it when he was checking out the other side of the Mitchell tube." She kissed her uncle's grizzled cheek and went to her truck.

She and Jake were going to catch a murderer. It was obvious Wilson had meant he'd seen her father years before, not recently. She'd known all along that was the likely explanation, but at least she'd learned a little more about her father today.

Chapter Seventeen

The sun was a golden orb in the sky as it sank over the mountain and into Lake Superior. Jake hunkered down behind a group of boulders with Skye. He'd thought to bring a blanket and a Thermos of coffee for the long night ahead, though he hoped the culprit would come out of hiding before dawn.

The light scent Skye wore wafted to his nose on the early evening breeze. He tried not to notice. There were too many things about her that appealed to him. Watching the breeze lift the tendrils of hair that escaped her long braid, he felt like a drowning man watching a passing ship. This feeling that burgeoned in his heart was something he'd never felt before.

How could he love her? He choked on his coffee as he pondered the problem.

"You okay?" Skye's dark brows winged upward and she patted him on the back.

"I'm fine." Being near her was a torture he both craved and feared. The blood thundered in his ears, and he looked away. He didn't want her to read the expression on his face. He felt like a rock atop Turtle Mountain—exposed to anyone who cared to look.

Skye didn't seem to notice he was antsy. She settled onto the blanket and took a sip of her coffee. "Uncle Louis says my father might be hiding out in that tunnel we saw the other day."

"It looked overgrown."

"I know, but maybe he was good at hiding it. I think I'll check it out tomorrow."

"Not alone, I hope."

She glanced at him and grinned. "Want to go with me?"

The thought made bile rise in this throat. He'd glanced inside and it was like a grave. "Not hardly."

"I didn't think so."

"Think you're smart, don't you?" He took her hand to prove to himself he could be near her and be unaffected. Her fingers curled around his in a way that made him feel like Paul Bunyan. Why was he so afraid of committing himself, of settling down in one place? Maybe it was a matter of trust, as Kimball had said. Jake liked being in control. Thinking about giving that up was like stepping off into an abyss. But maybe it was time he did just that.

Skye said God didn't want us to let fear rule, but he wasn't sure how to get past it. Maybe step into the abyss and admit his feelings.

The crunch of gravel brought his head up. He peered over the rock. "Someone's here."

Skye looked, too. "It's just Pop."

"Why do you call him Pop?"

She shrugged. "He's like a dad to me. He's tried really hard to fill the void my dad left. They were good friends."

Jake frowned. "Could Wilson be talking about James? Maybe he was confused. Has he ever heard you call James 'Pop'?"

"I don't know." She didn't want to believe it, but it made sense. It was the final death knell to her hopes. Her father hadn't come back. Wilson was just confused again.

The foreman went inside the mine, and Jake and Skye settled back to wait again. Jake kept possession of her hand, and she didn't protest. He had to say something or he would explode.

He lifted her hand to his lips and kissed her palm. He saw her shiver.

"Don't do that," she said. She didn't pull her hand away though.

He moved closer and trailed his other hand up her arm to her cheek. "You look beautiful in the moonlight." He told himself to just say the words.

"Why, you must say that to all the girls."

"You're my girl and the only one I want to say it to."

She went still, but he heard her catch her breath.

"Am I your girl? I hadn't realized." Her gaze searched his face.

It was now or never. "I've been fighting it for weeks, but I can't do it any longer. I realized tonight I love you, Skye. I didn't want to, but there it is." He rubbed his thumb over her bottom lip. The muscles in her neck moved as she swallowed.

Her eyes seemed to grow soft and luminous in the darkening twilight. "Are you having a joke on me?"

"It's not something I would joke about." He leaned forward, and his lips met hers. The sweetness of her breath mingled with the scent of pine from the needles under them. He closed his eyes and let the love wash over him. Why had he been so afraid of this moment?

She uttered a soft cry and wrapped her arms around his neck. The kiss seemed to last an eternity, then she pulled away and gave a gentle sigh. "I love you, too. I've loved you for weeks, I think, but I don't want to. We're too different. This isn't real."

"I'm not laughing," he whispered. "What I feel is real enough that I want to marry you."

Had he really said he wanted to marry her? He'd shocked himself, but he wasn't taking it back. They could work out their differences on the direction their dreams took.

"Marriage?" Her voice trembled. Her steady gaze locked onto his. It felt as though she looked deep into his soul. "Are you sure you can be happy living here?" Her breath whispered across his face.

He stiffened. "Can't we compromise? Part of the year here and part of the year on a new dig?"

Her face tightened. "What if my father comes back? I wouldn't want to leave him."

"Skye, you can't live your whole life waiting for your father."

She bit her lip. "I can't leave here, Jake."

One of them would have to be willing to give up a dream, he thought, as darkness fell over the mountain. One of them would have to have enough love to take a step back from what they thought they wanted.

He wasn't sure if he could. He watched her in the shadows, and the love he felt seemed to grow until his chest felt like it would burst. Still, he couldn't see staying here forever. He didn't understand her fear of leaving the island.

"We'll talk about it later," he said. She'd see reason. She had to.

Skye wanted to sing, to jump to her feet and dance across the tops of the peaks around her. Jake loved her. How could that be? Surely, he could be happy here if he tried. And she thought he wanted to try. He hadn't said he wouldn't stay. She allowed the hope to squelch the cold, hard reason that lay in the pit of her stomach. He didn't share her faith. They had to talk about that.

"Someone's coming," Jake's voice whispered in her ear.

"I didn't hear a car." She craned her neck to look.

"Stay down. Whoever it is sneaked up on foot." Jake pressed her back against the rock while he took a cautious peek.

She heard a soft footfall along the path that led past their hideout. A sidling, secretive sound that raised the hair along her back. Whoever it was didn't want to be seen or heard. The stealthy approach brought a sense of danger with it. For the first time, she questioned their sanity in trying to trap a killer.

He—or she—had shot at them, attacked them both and killed Cameron. What made them think they were smarter and stronger than the person with the cunning and treachery evidenced by the deeds over the past few weeks?

She couldn't stand it any longer. Shaking off Jake's restraint, she edged her head up to see who walked along the dark path. A hulking shadow loomed in the moonlight then passed them by. It was too dark to make out a face, but the figure moved like a man.

"Stay here," Jake whispered. "I can't tell who it is. I need to get a better look."

They moved up the path. Skye winced as their feet rattled the stones in the same stealthy manner as the man's had done. Surely he would hear them. Jake must have realized the same thing. He pointed at a widening in the path that held a boulder.

"Let's hide behind there and wait until he comes down."

She nodded and slipped behind the boulder with Jake. It seemed hours before they heard the faint movements again.

"Here he comes," Jake whispered.

Skye ducked her head, sure the man would see them in the bright moonlight. The sounds he made moved by again, and she peeked over the edge of the boulder. "He's got the eggs."

"We need to follow him." Jake took her hand and led her down the path. They took care to stay back from the man's tall form.

"We'll cut through the woods to the SUV."

Stumbling in the dark, they hurried to the SUV. Skye prayed the man wouldn't get away before they could follow him. They jumped in the SUV and pulled out of the hiding spot.

"Where would he have parked?"

"I'll show you." Skye directed him down an overgrown lane. Jake had the headlamps off so it was slow-going in the dark, even with the moon shining.

They rounded a curve and saw the glow of a car's lights disappearing around the corner. "There he is!" Skye leaned forward.

"I see him." Jake sped up a little. "We have to make sure he doesn't see us."

They kept the car in distant view.

"Any idea where he's going? This seems to be in the direction where we met up with Wilson."

"It is." Skye frowned. What could be in that meadow that was so important?

"Is there a shortcut where we could be waiting there for him when he arrives? That has to be where he's making for."

Skye thought a moment. "Maybe. We haven't had any rain lately so the creek might be dry enough to get across down another lane." She directed him on where to turn. "Put your headlights on. It should be safe enough now. Besides, we'll never stay on the path in the deep woods without some light."

Jake nodded and flipped on the lights. The beams pushed back the edge of darkness to a few feet, but the looming black of the deep woods seemed foreboding. Shrubs scraped along the side of the SUV like bony fingers.

Skye wanted to be anywhere but here. She blinked and strained to see more than the few feet illuminated by the headlights.

A pull-off suddenly looked familiar. "Here. Stop here!" She pointed and Jake steered the SUV into a small area barely large enough for the vehicle.

He killed the engine. "We'd better hurry."

Skye nodded and swung open her door, wincing when brambles scratched along the paint. An owl hooted overhead, and she smelled the musty scent of wet leaves and mud from the nearly dry creek bed just off to her right.

"Through here." She took Jake's hand, flipped on her flashlight, and led him over slippery stones that peeked up through the few inches of water still in the creek. He nearly lost his balance on one moss-covered rock but recovered before he landed in the water.

Skye felt like a lumbering moose as they fought their way through the inky darkness to the clearing she knew was there somewhere. Something large thrashed in the brush to their left and her skin tightened. The last thing she would want to do is to run into a bear in the dark.

"What's that?" Jake whispered. His fingers tightened on hers.

"Make some noise." She raised her voice and began to sing "Amazing Grace." Jake chimed in with her. The noise faded.

"I hope we didn't scare the guy off," she said, tugging at Jake's hand. "Hurry."

They broke through the final barrier of brush into the meadow. The moon made it seem as though they'd stepped from night into day. Skye looked around for a place to hide.

Jake pointed to the lean-to. "Behind there?"

She shook her head. "He might be heading for there." She pulled him toward the mine tunnel.

"Not in there!" He dug in his heels.

"No, no. Not the tunnel. But this brush pile is thick to the side of it. And he can't slip up behind us, either."

He nodded, his gaze wandering to the tunnel. She crouched behind the shrubs and tugged him down as they heard thrashing from the edge of the clearing.

"Here he comes." She ducked her head then peeked up high enough to see.

Peter stepped into the meadow. His shoulders bowed with the weight of the rocks he carried. Skye sucked in her breath. What was he doing here?

"He's got the eggs," Jake whispered. "You know, I thought it was going to be James."

"James?"

"Well, you call him Pop."

Skye was barely listening. What would Peter be doing with the eggs? How could he be involved with this? Maybe Wilson had told him where the eggs were and he was moving them for safekeeping.

They watched Peter stagger toward the lean-to.

"Maybe the rest of the eggs are in the lean-to," she mouthed to Jake. He nodded and started to stand, but she pulled him back. "Wait," she whispered.

Peter walked on by the lean-to toward where they crouched. He dropped the eggs onto the ground in front of the tunnel then reached forward and pulled the brambles from in front of the opening. They came easily, and Skye realized they'd been arranged there to hide the fact there had been recent activity in the tunnel.

If he pulled many more, he might take some of the ones they hid behind. She prayed for him to stop. She buried her face in her hands so he wouldn't see.

When Peter was gone, she was going to investigate. She had her flashlight in her pocket. Skye squeezed her eyes shut. Surely Peter had a good reason for what he'd done.

She opened her eyes and peeked up again. Jake's fingers closed in a warning grip around her own. She gave a reassuring squeeze back.

Peter picked up the eggs one by one and stuffed them into the mine opening, reaching in and sticking them off to one side. When he was done, he stood and dusted his hands then walked away toward the lean-to.

They watched until Peter turned to exit the clearing. Skye listened until the rustling faded, then stood and rushed to the mine opening. She pulled back the brush and shined her light inside. "Here, you hold the light while I get the eggs." She handed the flashlight to Jake, then crawled into the mine tunnel.

Grunting with the weight, she passed the eggs out to Jake. "Hand me the light a minute. I want to make sure I got them all."

She took the light and focused the beam into the deeper recesses of the tunnel. A lurid figure leaped into view. A scarecrow figure with leering teeth. Though it had startled her, she quickly realized it was put there to frighten. This must be the Spider Woman Wilson saw. Cobwebs hung from the arms and head. It was so obviously fake, she wondered how Wilson was taken in by it.

She backed away and saw a recent break in a wall. It must have happened when the explosion happened. She poked around and shoved a few boulders out of the way, then moved deeper into the tunnel and shone her light around again.

A heap of clothing back in a small niche caught her eye. "What is that?" she muttered.

"What's wrong?" Jake stooped and peered inside, though he didn't follow her in.

"Hang on a minute." She crawled toward the clothing. As she got closer, she froze when her gaze lit on bones. Human bones still clothed with jeans and a flannel shirt. She swept the light over the figure.

"No," she whispered. Horror closed her throat, and she struggled to scream past the constriction. Her gaze took in the bloodstains on the shirt and the knife still sticking from the chest.

Her father's chest.

Gasping and mewling, she backpedaled away from the sight.

"Skye, what is it?" Jake was beside her in the mine.

"There." She pointed. Shudders wracked her.

Jake took the flashlight and swept it over the figure. "Let's get out of here." His voice echoed off the walls of the tunnel.

She let him pull her from the enclosure, her mind still not registering what she'd seen. She had to be wrong, but she knew she was right. It was her father's remains.

"You're all right, I've got you." Jake drew her to her feet in the sweet, clean air.

She drew in a deep breath as he hugged her to his chest. She dropped the light on the ground.

"Can you talk about it?"

"It—it's my dad. He's in there." She shuddered, still unable to believe her own eyes. "He's dead."

"It's not your dad. It can't be. That poor soul has been dead a long time."

"No, you don't understand. He's wearing the clothes he wore the day he disappeared. He never deserted us. He was killed."

She clasped her arms around herself. "Peter killed my father."

Chapter Eighteen

"I'm sorry you had to see that. I thought I'd get here before you showed up."

Jake whirled at the voice. Peter stood right behind them, his right hand holding a pistol.

Gone were the gentle tones Jake had heard the man use with Skye. She was staring at Peter as if she'd never seen him before.

"Who are you?" she whispered. "The Peter I know wouldn't do this."

Jake looked down the bore of the gun. His gaze traveled up Peter's arm to his face and saw the flat stare of a man who had nothing to lose. Jake tensed and his thoughts whirled as he tried to figure out how to save Skye and himself from the man holding the gun.

"You killed him, didn't you? You killed my father." She shuddered, and tears trickled from her eyes.

"He'd always taken what I wanted. Always." Peter's eyes glittered in the moonlight. "Your mother was engaged to me first. You never knew that, did you?"

"You were my dad's best friend." Skye shook her head, her eyes clouded.

"I'd finally had enough. He taunted me one last time with what he had and I didn't. When he found the diamonds, it was the final straw."

"He found the diamonds?" Her mouth dropped open. "In the Mitchell tube! You caused the explosion so I wouldn't find them, didn't you?"

Peter shrugged. "The tunnel was unstable and our scuffle caused a cave-in. I couldn't dig him out without causing more cave-ins."

"So you had to keep me from opening Mitchell tube."

"Your mother meant more to me than the diamonds. I had enough money for us."

"So you just didn't want me to find my father's body. That's why you wouldn't let me open the tube. If I'd gone far enough with the extraction, you would have been exposed." She shook her head. "But why did you hire an assayer?" She put her hand over her mouth. "You hired him to tell me there weren't any diamonds, right? So I'd give up the search."

Peter's eyes hardened. "I've loved you like a daughter, Skye, but I can't let you take everything from me. Both of you, move into the tunnel."

"So *you* shot at us, put the snake in my truck, all of it?" Skye's voice was thick with tears.

"Let's say I commissioned a little help. It was easy to flame Tallulah's hatred. And Cameron was too greedy." He held out his hand. "I'll take my key back."

"Your key?" Skye pulled it slowly from her pocket.

"When you mentioned it at dinner, I knew I'd better get it back. Fingerprints and all that." Peter snatched it from her hand, then smiled and motioned with the gun. "Now move into the tunnel."

Jake was shaking his head before Peter finished talking. No way was he going in that tight space. He'd shocked himself by going inside when Skye fell apart. He clenched his fists. Better to die out here under the open sky.

His muscles coiled to spring forward, but before he could think, Peter stepped forward and thumped him across the forehead. He pitched forward, darkness descending too quickly to resist.

Skye's numbness broke as she saw Jake sag to the ground. "No!" She launched herself toward Peter, and they both tumbled to the ground. "Don't hurt him."

Peter tossed her off like she weighed nothing, then was on his feet in an instant. The gun was pointed at

Jake. "I'd love to drill loverboy," he said. "Give me a reason and he's dead."

She drew in a deep breath and sat up. "I'll be good. Don't hurt him."

"I loved you, Skye." He looked genuinely remorseful. "I tried to scare you into shutting down the mine, and I tried to get rid of Baxter so it would never come to this. It's going to kill your mother."

"What are you going to do?"

He motioned with the gun. "Drag him into the shaft."

"No! He hates caves."

"What a shame," he said, a sarcastic edge to his voice. "Loverboy has a flaw. Do what I say or I'll put a bullet in his brain, and he'll never be afraid again."

He would do it, too. She could see it in the flat stare he gave. No redeeming emotion lingered there. He was a man determined to do what had to be done.

She got slowly to her feet and moved toward Jake. There had to be some way out of this.

"Get a move on," Peter said sharply.

She grabbed Jake by the shoulders and began to drag him into the mine opening. He was a big man and hard to move. Rivulets of perspiration had ran down her face and her back by the time she'd managed to get him into the tunnel.

It was pitch-black inside the mine. The flashlight was on Jake's belt, but she didn't dare turn it on. Peter might take it from her, and she didn't think she could bear to be without light of any kind.

She propped Jake against the wall and turned to plead

with Peter again. Feeling her way, she moved toward the mouth of the tunnel when a great explosion knocked her to the ground.

Jake swam slowly up from the dark. Where was he? Blinking his eyes, he smelled the dank odor of earth. Damp crept along his bones, and he felt a hard rock poking his ribs.

"Jake, Jake, wake up." Skye was shaking his shoulder, and he realized he'd been hearing her for some time.

He moved his head and groaned as a shaft of pure agony shot along the right side of his face and centered in his ear. He rubbed his head and felt a sticky goose egg under his hair. "Where are we?"

"Don't freak, okay?" She helped him to sit up, and he leaned against what felt like rock to his back. Memory came flooding back. Peter. The gun. He groaned as another wave of pain and nausea swept over him.

"Where's Peter?"

"He's gone." Skye rubbed his back. "I wish I had some feverfew for your head," she fretted.

Jake froze as he opened his eyes as wide as he could and still saw nothing but total darkness. "Am I blind?"

"No, no." She paused. "At least I don't think so."

"Why is it so dark?" He put out a groping hand, wanting light with the desperation of a drowning man seeking a life jacket. His hand touched Skye's arm, and he gripped it.

"We—we're in the mine shaft." Skye put her arms around him.

He clung to her as the words sank in. Panic began to play at the edges of his reason. "Let's get out of here!" He felt along the rock wall, seeking an opening.

"Peter caved in the opening. An explosion of some kind. It's bad, Jake. I don't see any way out."

He heard fear and panic in Skye's voice, and it brought his mind into focus. He had to stay calm, had to save them both. Hugging her tightly to his chest, he patted her hair. "It's okay, we'll figure a way out."

She gave a shaky breath and nodded. "We have the flashlight. It was on your belt. I didn't want to use it until you woke up."

"How long was I out?" His chest felt tight.

"About an hour, I think." Skye sounded a little calmer.

The air smelled stale and dank, and Jake's throat tightened even more as he tried to draw in his breath in lungs that felt too large for his chest. *Help me, Lord.* "What's the verse you told me once—the one about not being afraid."

Skye was silent a moment then she recited in a voice that gained strength as she went along, "God has not given us a spirit of fear, but of power and a sound mind."

He fastened all his hope on that verse, and felt a lightness spread through him. In this dark place, God's promises were the only illumination they had. And he was finding out more and more, that was all he needed.

"Let's pray for that sound mind right now. God knows we're here. He'll help us figure out what to do." They held hands while Jake prayed for courage and strength. He asked God to take charge of their lives. As he prayed, he felt the panic receding and a calmness he didn't know he possessed took charge of his limbs. Why had he been so afraid of this?

"Here's the flashlight." Skye pressed the cold, hard tube of the flashlight into his hand.

The comforting feel of the grip and the solid heft of the light encouraged him. He flipped it on and shone the light around the area. The panic threatened again when he saw how closed in they were.

"Got any idea how to get out of here?" He swallowed back the panic, praying silently again for courage. The sharp edge of his fear began to dull again, little by little.

"Turn the light off a minute and let me think."

Turn the light off. Was she nuts? He gripped the ribbed tube of the flashlight. No way was he going back into the dark.

"We need to conserve the light." Skye grabbed the flashlight and switched it off.

The tunnel plunged into darkness, and Jake's stomach plunged with it. His lungs squeezed tight, and he gasped.

"Breathe," Skye said, taking his hand. "I'm right here. And so is God."

"I know," he croaked. He forced air past the constriction in his windpipe. The dots in front of his eyes settled down.

"This main tunnel used to connect with the Mitchell tube," she said. "That's caved in now."

"Are there any other tunnels leading down a minor tube? Or is there anything in here to dig with? Maybe we can get out that way." His muscles bunched, eager to do something, anything.

"I don't know. Let's explore." She handed the light back to him.

He flipped it on. The sudden infusion of light brought hope with it. He told himself not to look at the sloping walls and the low ceiling. Standing, he took Skye's hand, and they walked toward where the tunnel turned. He had to bend over to avoid hitting his head on the ceiling.

They wandered for what seemed like hours down the tight tunnel until they finally came to a cave-in. The light was dimming, and he glanced at his watch. It had only been twenty minutes.

"Better turn it off again."

He knew she was right, but he froze at her request. Finally moving his stiff thumb, he flipped it off. It seemed hopeless. There was no way out. His nerves felt on fire, as though he would burst into flame at any minute. Skye was depending on him. They had to get out.

No one would miss them until morning. His family all knew they'd intended to stake out the dig all night. They wouldn't come looking until at least noon tomorrow, he guessed. They'd look at the dig, and there would be nothing to guide them to this remote spot.

"How deep is the rockfall? Could anyone hear us tomorrow if we banged right here?"

"I don't think so. The cave-in covered a lot of area. We could try though." She slipped cold fingers into his. "I'm tired. Can we sit and rest a while?"

The last thing he wanted was to just sit and ignore the problem, but he squeezed her hand. "Sure."

He sat beside her on the cold, dank earth again. She shivered, and he slipped his arm around her. "I wish I had my jacket."

"Your arm will do."

She snuggled against his side, and he leaned his head on her hair. Entwined like this, their situation didn't seem quite so dire, but he knew he was kidding himself. Death by starvation and dehydration wasn't a pleasant thought.

"We're going to die, aren't we?" Skye's voice was too quiet and soft, tinged with resignation.

"No, we'll find a way out." He forced conviction into his voice. She was depending on him to stay strong, to keep them focused.

"I'm okay with it. At least we'll be together." Her fingers tightened against his shirt. "I can say this now in the dark. I never thought I could love a man like I love you. You're everything I ever dreamed of, Jake. I wish we could have had all those years, raised children together, fought and loved and dreamed. I think I could even have left the island for you." Her voice grew choked.

A ball of emotion formed in his throat. "We'll have

that yet, my sweet Skye. I'm not giving up." Determination replaced fear. He wanted all those things with this woman. "If we get out of here, you won't have to leave the island. I'll stay here and work on the dig here. That should last me a lot of years."

Funny how that sacrifice seemed so small now that they were faced with death. Reality had a funny way of putting things in perspective.

She leaned up and kissed his jaw. He found her face in the dark and rubbed his thumb over her high cheekbones, along the silky fall of her hair. Leaning down, he kissed her, a lingering caress that fueled his resolve. "I love you," he whispered. "So much. My life was empty before I met you."

She returned his kiss then burrowed her face against his chest again. They sat like that for several long moments, then he kissed the top of her head and released her. "We've got to find a way out."

He stood and pulled her to her feet. Flipping on the flashlight again, he shone it around the tight confines. The light only illuminated smooth walls. Then he spied a shadow along the floor of one wall.

"What's that?" He stepped closer. "Looks like a crawl space." He got on his hands and knees and peered under. "I can't see anything. It's too small for me to crawl under."

"Let me try." Skye got on her belly and stuck her head and arms through the opening. "Hand me the light." Her voice was muffled.

He slipped the flashlight into her hand and she pulled

it to the other side. She could see a faint illumination from the other room. "I think I see outside—looks like moonlight! And there's a box here."

"What's in it?"

A faint scraping sound came to his ears. "Explosives, I think. They must be what Peter used to blow up the Mitchell tube." Her head reemerged. "I can't get the box through here, but I can get some dynamite."

"Can you get through to the other side?"

She shook her head. "It's too tight." She stuck her head through again.

There was more scraping and banging from the other side of the wall. "I've almost got it," she panted. She wiggled as she struggled with whatever was on the other side of the wall. "Got it!" She backed out of the hole and triumphantly held up two sticks of dynamite.

"Was that all there was?" He took the dynamite from her. "It's a little damp. I hope it's stable." Decaying dynamite gave off nitroglycerin and could be dangerous.

"It's all we've got. We could try blowing this hole big enough to get through."

He thought a minute. Stuck in this small tunnel, it would be dangerous. But at least they'd be dead quickly instead of lingering with starvation and dehydration. "It might work, but it also might seal us in even tighter." That was the biggest worry.

"What do we have to lose?"

Exactly his thought. "I've got a pocketknife. We might be able to chip away enough of the hole for you to squeeze through. You could go for help." The thought of being in this coffin alone made it hard to speak, but he had to get Skye to safety.

"We'd be dead before we could chip that much away," she said. "Let's go together or not at all."

"Is there a longer fuse in that box?"

"I'll look." She crouched down again and wedged herself under the opening again. "There's some fuse and matches as well." She backed out and handed the booty to him.

"We could put as long a fuse on it as possible then get far back. Let's start with just one stick of dynamite. I don't know much about explosives so we'd better play it safe."

"Sounds good to me."

Skye's cheerful voice brought a smile to his face. She could find a silver lining in the darkest cloud. He knew it was a long shot, but there was no reason to discourage her.

"Okay, you hold the light." He stretched the fuse out and attached it to a stick of the explosive. He put the dynamite in the opening to the other room. "Let's start backing up."

Skye nodded, and they began to move away from the opening. They reached a bend in the tunnel, but the fuse wouldn't reach around it. "You go around the curve. I'll join you when the fuse is lit."

"I want to stay with you."

"I'll be right there. I can move faster if I know you're safe."

She huffed but did as he said. The area plunged into darkness. Rats, he couldn't see the fuse. He fumbled with the matches but couldn't see well enough to strike one properly.

"Bring the light here a minute," he said.

Skye moved toward him. "I knew you needed me." She focused the beam on his hands.

Jake knelt and struck the match against the rock beside him. It flared and died. "I think they're wet."

"Try again."

Skye had found only four matches. He swiped the next match on the rock, and it did nothing but fizzle. "Only two more," he said.

"It will work."

The fervency in her voice steadied his hand. The third match broke in his hand.

She put her hand over his. "This is our last shot. It has to work. I've been praying."

Holding the match close to the sulphur so it wouldn't break, he held his breath and struck it against the rock. It flared to life. The flame began to sputter and he quickly held it to the fuse. Just as it died, the fuse caught.

"Thank You, God!" Skye clapped her hands together.

"Get back!" He grabbed her by the shoulders and pushed her around the corner and to the ground. They both fell against the hard dirt, and he covered her with his body. "Please, God," he said softly. He glanced over his shoulder and could see a dim glow as the fire raced along the fuse.

The explosion came in a soft *whumph* that washed over them. Jake could feel the pressure in his ears, then a wind rushed past them. Rubble rattled to the floor, and small stones rained down on them. Jake covered his head with his hands and made sure Skye was protected.

As the dust settled, he lifted his head. The flashlight had gone out, and as he picked it up, he heard the rattle of broken glass. There would be no second chance.

"Are you all right?" He rolled off Skye onto the ground and sat up.

"I'm fine. Are you hurt?"

"I don't think so." His back stung from the small stones that had struck him, but he would live. At least for now. He helped her to her feet. "The light is busted. We'll have to find the hole in the dark."

They rounded the curve in the tunnel. "I think I see it!" Skye moved away from him.

"Wait, it might not be stable." He caught at her hand and pulled her behind him. "Let me check it out first." Running his hands over the walls, he made his way to where moonlight cast a glow too weak to see with. It was more an impression of light rather than a real illumination.

As he neared the spot, he could see the hole was larger, at least large enough for Skye to exit through. "We've done it!" He swung her into his arms and hugged her. His throat closed with gratitude to God.

Skye kissed him and turned to peer under the hole. "Let's get out of here."

"You go first." He went down on one knee and glanced through the opening.

Skye went to her belly and slithered through the hole. "Plenty of room."

The thought of going through that tiny hole nearly made him vomit. He had to do this though. He got to his stomach and began to wiggle into the opening. He could feel the rough edges of rock tear at his arms. His skin burned where the stones scraped him raw.

The hole narrowed farther, and panic flared again. He forced himself forward, then his shoulders caught and wedged. Caught, trapped. He fought the vise around his body. It was like being swallowed alive by a python.

"It's got me!" He could see nothing, feel nothing, but the tight embrace of the rock walls.

Chapter Nineteen

Skye heard the panic in Jake's voice and turned to help. She could barely see his face in the dim moonlight that came from the opening to the outside. She touched his clammy forehead. "I'm here. We'll get you out."

"It's too tight." He panted and tried to twist free.

"Stop struggling." She ran her hands across his shoulders and into the hole that held him fast. Maybe there was wiggle room somewhere. "Try to drop your left shoulder."

He was gasping so hard she didn't see how he could hear her. This had to be a nightmare for him with his fear of tight spaces, though prayer had kept him calmer than she ever dreamed possible. She knelt and placed her palms on each side of his face. "It's okay, Jake. There's room. Drop your left shoulder."

He nodded and she ran her hands across his shoulders again. "Here, drop your arm a bit so your shoulder moves." She felt the muscles bunch under her hands as he tried to do as she said. The left shoulder dropped a couple of inches. "You've got it!" She grabbed his arms and began to tug.

At first he seemed to be wedged tighter than ever, then she felt a little movement and he began to move forward. Moments later, he was lying on the floor panting. Drawing in great lungfuls of air, he rolled to his back. Moonlight touched his face, and she saw he was as pale as the white light coming through the opening.

She held out her hand. "Let's get out of here."

He grabbed her hand and she helped him to his feet. They went through the final opening into the light. Fresh air had never tasted so sweet. She drew in a deep breath tinged with pine from the thick hemlock forest all around them.

"Where is this place? Does it look familiar?" Jake slipped his arm around her.

"Not really." The hemlocks hemmed them in, and she couldn't see much of the terrain in the faint glimmer of moonlight.

Jake glanced at the sky. "There's the North Star. I'd say the road is this way." He took her hand and led her toward an opening in the trees.

Half an hour later, they stumbled out of the trees and onto the road. "I know where we are now!" She pointed to a road sign. "About five miles down there is where Sheriff Mitchell lives."

"He won't be pleased to have us pounding on his door at—" He stopped and peered at his watch. "Four in the morning."

"Who cares?" She felt like dancing in the road. This nightmare was almost over. Except for confronting Peter and telling her mother what he'd done. Her jubilation faded.

Jake seemed to sense her disquiet because he paused and pulled her into his arms. "It will be okay," he whispered. "Peter can't hurt you anymore."

"He already has." She rubbed her fists against her eyes. "I can't bear to tell Mother what he's done."

"At least you know what happened to your father. You'll have closure on that—your mother, too."

She nodded. "I suppose I always knew he was never coming back. Deep down where I didn't bring it out to admit it."

He kissed her and the caress held all the promise of the future they'd almost been deprived of. "Let's get out of here. We have a wedding to plan."

"You've never even proposed."

"I'll remedy that right now." He dropped to his knees in the middle of the road and took her hand. "I'm not going anywhere until you say yes."

"Someone will run over you there." She giggled, her

fear and sorrow dropping away.

"As long as you say yes, I'll die happy." He smiled up at her. The moonlight highlighted the face she had come to love against her will.

"Yes." She cupped his face in her palms and leaned down to kiss him. "Now let's get out of here."

He stood and dug his pocketknife out. He flipped a blade out and cut a small twig from the baby hemlock tree just off the road. Coiling it into a circle, he slipped it onto her finger. "This will have to do until I can buy you a proper ring."

She closed her hand around the makeshift ring. "I might not let you take it back." A burgeoning happiness threatened to overwhelm her with tears. She'd heard about people crying from happiness, and now she knew how that felt.

He embraced her again. "Wynne will be smug and self-satisfied," he said. "She predicted you were going to batter down my defenses."

"It was the other way around." She pulled away and slipped her arm into his as they proceeded down the road.

Skye stood behind the sheriff as he pounded on her mother's door. She wouldn't be able to go through with the accusation if Jake weren't right here with her. How did she tell her mother her husband was a murderer?

Peter opened the door. His eyes widened when he saw her and Jake standing behind Sheriff Mitchell. "You!" He took a step back and turned to run.

"Peter Metis, you're under arrest for the murder of Harry Blackbird." The sheriff stepped through the door and clapped handcuffs on Peter.

"No, you've got it all wrong." Tears came to Peter's eyes.

"Peter? What's wrong?" Skye's mother came down the hall in her terry housecoat and slippers. Her face went white when she saw her husband in handcuffs. "What's going on?"

"It's a long story, Mother." Skye stepped around the sheriff and led her mother into the living room.

It was nearly an hour later before her mother was calm enough to drink the coffee Jake brought in. "I always knew Peter was jealous of Harry. They fought over me like wolverines in high school. He masked his real nature well." Her mother rubbed her eyes.

Skye patted her mother's hand. She didn't know what to say. Peter's treachery was beyond belief.

Her mother's gaze went from her to Jake. "You two finally got things settled, didn't you?" She gave a slight smile.

Jake's dark eyes slid to Skye's face, and she smiled to see the love and possessiveness there. "Yes, we did. See my ring?" She held out her evergreen ring.

Her mother's eyes filled with tears. "It's going to be hard planning a wedding with this hanging over our heads. But maybe it will give me something else to think about."

"We'll get through it, Mother." Skye squeezed her mother's hand. She glanced at her watch. "We need to tell Jake's family what's happened, too. They're probably at breakfast now."

"Go along, I'll be fine." Her mother dabbed at her eyes.

Skye hated to leave her, but she kissed her mother's soft cheek and rose. "Get some rest. I'll check back later."

Her mother nodded. "I'll try to lie down, but I'll never sleep." Her lips trembled.

Skye bit her lip and followed Jake outside. "It seems awful to be so happy when things are going to be so hard for my mother."

"Would you rather we put the wedding off for a while?"

She laughed. "I can tell by the way you said it, you don't want that."

"I don't. But I want you happy."

"I'm happy." She smiled to drive home her statement. "I don't want to wait. I feel I've been waiting for you all my life."

"I know I've been waiting for you." He drew her into his arms under the canopy of five dreamcatchers on the porch above their heads. "You've been the one who has haunted my dreams all my life. Now that I've caught you, I'm never letting go."

"I wouldn't have it any other way," she said, bringing his lips down to meet hers.